AMISH CHRISTMAS ABDUCTION

DANA R. LYNN

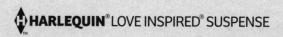

HARLEQUIN® LOVE INSPIRED® SUSPENSE

LOVE INSPIRED BOOKS

Recycling programs
for this product may
not exist in your area.

ISBN-13: 978-0-373-67867-9

Amish Christmas Abduction

www.Harlequin.com

Printed in U.S.A.

The sound terrified her.

The child's scream.

She shot up the stairs, wishing Paul were here.

The child shrieked again and a voice growled, "Shut up or I'll do it for you."

Irene crept down the hall and saw him. The man she'd have nightmares about. As he lunged at her, she grabbed a vase and slammed it into his head. He staggered, giving her the moment she needed to grab the child.

"Irene!"

Paul! He'd come to save her!

As the man pulled a gun, Irene rushed into the bedroom and locked the door. From out in the hall she heard gunfire, a crash. Then quiet.

Her fear subsided when Paul busted open the door. From the look on his face, she knew the gunman had gotten away.

"I'm bringing the child home with me."

She waited for the argument. Instead, he nodded. "We'll keep a detail at your house."

Then his face went ashen. "Irene, this isn't over. They're after the child, and because you're the only witness, you." Sh[...]

keep killing till t[...]

Dana R. Lynn grew up in Illinois. She met a man at a wedding who she told her parents was her future husband. Nineteen months later, they were married. Today they live in rural Pennsylvania with their three children, two dogs, one cat, one rabbit, one horse and six chickens. In addition to writing, she works as an educational interpreter for the deaf and is active in several ministries in her church.

Books by Dana R. Lynn

Love Inspired Suspense

Amish Country Justice

Plain Target
Plain Retribution
Amish Christmas Abduction

Presumed Guilty
Interrupted Lullaby

Visit the Author Profile page at Harlequin.com.

Blessed are they that mourn, for they shall be comforted.
–Matthew 5:4

Rachael, Bradley and Gregory.
There is not a day that I don't thank God for the blessing
of being your mom. Love you forever.

Brad...thanks for loving me and encouraging me
to live my dream. Love you!

Acknowledgments

To my family and friends, who supported me
and held me up in prayer...I appreciate you so much.
Thank you with all my heart.

To my editor, Elizabeth Mazer...thank you
for all your guidance. It's a joy to work with you.

To my agent, Tamela Hancock Murray...
thanks for believing in me. I am grateful
for all your efforts on my behalf.

To my Lord and Savior...thank You for Your presence
in my life. I am nothing without You.

ONE

"Didn't you see the sign? This is private property."

Irene Martello stepped back from the door, her raised hand falling to her side... The man who answered the door glared at her. It was the most vicious stare she'd ever encountered. Anger at being treated so rudely warred with apprehension. She was here alone...unprotected. Would this man turn violent?

"I'm sorry to bother you," she managed. "I was trying to find the Zilcher residence."

She shivered as he glowered, his heavy brows lowering over black eyes. It was difficult to see his mouth through the thick black beard, but she had the distinct impression he was scowling.

"You have the wrong house. They live there." He jerked his head sharply toward the house next door.

"Sorry..." She opened her mouth to apologize for any inconvenience, but stopped when there was a movement behind Black Beard. A young woman, somewhere in her late teens or early twenties, stood in an open doorway deeper inside the house. As the man whirled around and speared her with a glance, she fled back out of sight. Was that a child crying? Irene leaned forward instinctively, straining to hear. He returned that glare to Irene, and she straightened again. It was none of her business if he had children, she chastised herself. He narrowed his eyes at her, and she felt true fear at the way his eyes blazed at her.

Turning on her heel, she moved briskly back down the steps. Only the fact that the ground was covered with snow kept her from running as she hightailed it back to her SUV. After getting in, she started the engine with a shaking hand, then backed along the driveway and onto the dirt road. She drove past the mailboxes on the side of the road and realized that what she'd thought was a 1 had actually been a 7. A natural mistake to make.

In no time, she was in the driveway of the correct house. She fumbled around for her purse and laptop bag, completely aware that the man had moved outside and was watching her from his porch.

After pushing open the door of her SUV,

Irene stepped from the vehicle, glad she'd opted for warmth rather than fashion as her heavy boots crunched the snow beneath them. Against her better judgment, she peeked at the man from house number seven. She instantly regretted it. His face had darkened even more. Turning quickly, her face heated as she felt his glare continuing to bore into her back. She took a deep breath, refusing to admit to herself how unsettling her encounter with the man had been.

Trying to appear calm, she pulled her belongings from the dark red SUV and shut the door with her hip. Slammed it, actually. Even though she refused to look, she was aware that he was still there. Now she was getting mad. Why was he watching her like that? What did he expect? That she'd drive back over to chat? Not likely.

Enough! She had a job to do. A job she loved, even though she'd only been working with the Early Intervention program for two months. Today she was meeting a new family. She shifted the red bag carrying both the laptop and her file of papers for the family to sign.

Determined, she made her way up the narrow walkway to the small house, careful to avoid looking at the man on the porch. It didn't help matters any that the family had requested a late meeting, due to the father's work schedule. It was already going on four o'clock. By the time the meeting ended, it would be almost five. LaMar Pond started getting dark around that time in December. At least it was Friday. After this appointment, she could pick up her own kids and enjoy a quiet evening at home.

Come on, Irene. One more home visit, then you're all done.

Once, only once, did she glance to the right. Her eyes switched targets as she became aware of movement from the side window. The same young woman she'd seen in the house was peering out of the blinds. She had the most hopeless face Irene had ever seen.

Something wasn't right.

The door in front of Irene opened. Taking her eyes off the creepy house, she forced herself to smile at the young couple waiting anxiously. For now, she needed to focus on work. But as soon as she was done with the meeting, she had every intention of calling her brother, Lieutenant Jace Tucker, and filling him in on the house and the woman. If her instincts were correct—and they usually were—that was a woman who needed help.

It might be nothing. But Irene knew she wouldn't rest easy until she had called. Maybe Jace wouldn't be able to do anything, but there was always the possibility that the police would keep a closer eye on the area.

Irene was very familiar with the police. Not only was her older brother a lieutenant, but she'd been married to a cop for six years, six wonderful years, before he'd been killed in the line of duty a little over three years ago.

The familiar ache in her chest when she thought of Tony was almost comforting.

Once inside the warm house, she was escorted into the dining room. She focused on the young family. The little boy she was there to evaluate was adorable, his little head bald except for a light fuzz. He was almost two years old, and had just been diagnosed with a vision impairment. Irene's job as the service coordinator was to decide if the child qualified for Early Intervention services. The meeting was merely a formality. Having a diagnosis almost always guaranteed that he would receive services.

In less than an hour, the meeting was completed and Irene was pushing her feet back into her winter boots.

"I will call you when I have the IFSP meeting scheduled," she told the mother, referring to the Individualized Family Service Plan meeting with the family and the therapists who would become part of the little boy's team.

After bidding the Zilchers goodbye, she pulled

the door open and stepped outside. It had started to snow while she was inside. She tried to keep her focus on her car, but it was no use. The other house drew her gaze like a magnet.

The man was probably still home. There were three vehicles in the driveway—a truck, a Jeep and a small sedan. But no one was standing outside. The man must have gone inside.

Relief coursed through her. And quite a bit of embarrassment. Imagine getting so upset because someone was watching her! What a goose she was! It wasn't like he had threatened her or anything like that.

Getting to her car, she frowned. Her door wasn't locked. She must have been so rattled by that man that she'd forgotten to lock it. She shrugged. It wasn't out of the norm to leave doors unlocked in LaMar Pond, especially out on the back roads. She had friends who didn't even lock their house doors at night.

She quickly climbed into the car and shut the door, making sure to lock it the moment she was inside. After starting the car, she turned up the heat to help rid herself of some of the chill, not all of which was from the weather. Lifting her head, she froze.

There, in the Zilcher family's front room window, a large Christmas tree sparkled and shimmered. The tree hadn't been lit when she'd arrived or she would have noticed it, no matter how freaked-out she had been. It was probably on an automatic timer. It was beautiful, looking at it through the snow. She swallowed the lump in her throat. She wasn't looking forward to Christmas, just a few weeks away. It would be the third since Tony's death. Her boys would go through another holiday without their father. A father little Matthew hardly remembered. He'd only been two. Now he was five. Seven-year-old AJ had more memories, but had forgotten so many details. It broke her heart.

A soft ping signaled an incoming text. Irene sighed. And this would be her mom, asking her to attend late-night services with her and the family on Christmas Eve. Just like Irene used to do every year before God abandoned her and her babies. She glanced at her phone. Oh, yeah. Just as she thought. She would hear about it later, but she was going to just ignore the text. For now.

A door slammed. Startled, her head jerked up in the direction of the sound. It had come from the man's house.

He was back, his eyes burning with anger. She could almost feel the menace emanating from him. Thankfully, he wasn't looking at her. He appeared to be searching for something, though, as his dark gaze swept over his yard.

Dropping her phone, Irene put her car into Reverse and started to back out of the driveway. Thankfully, there was no traffic on the road, so she could pull onto the street, away from the man, without waiting. But moments later, she heard a shout.

He was running her way!

Panicked now, she jerked the gearshift into Drive and peeled out. The vehicle fishtailed. Her grip tightened on the wheel. It straightened out and she continued, exhaling in relief.

Steering her SUV up the hill, she drove as fast as she dared before braking for the stop sign at the T on top of the hill. There was only one car coming. She edged her car forward, ready to turn right. She waited for the other driver to pass, drumming her fingers nervously on the steering wheel.

Come on. Come on.

Her back windshield shattered.

Irene screamed. What had just happened? A look in the rearview mirror confirmed her nightmare. The pickup truck she'd seen in the neighbor's drive was right on her bumper, and the man with the black beard was leaning out the window, some sort of rifle in his hand. She wasn't going to give him the chance to take a second shot. She shoved her foot down on the gas and whipped her car forward. She drove as fast as she could. She couldn't stop now to call the police. If she didn't concentrate on getting out of here, he'd get her for sure. But the moment she could pull over...

She heard a roar behind her. A glance in the mirror showed the pickup was coming up on her bumper. It was moving faster than she was, dangerously fast given the slick condition of the roads.

Now would be a good time to pray...if she still did that.

Since she didn't, she was on her own.

The truck slammed into the back of her SUV. She shrieked and pushed her foot down as hard as she dared on the gas pedal. She had never been so grateful for four-wheel drive. Pushing her foot down a little farther, the SUV lurched as it sped up. The truck stayed on her tail, then slammed into her again. Her SUV went into a full spin and slid off the road into a ditch. She was stuck.

Tears tracked down her cheeks. She was going to die! Her babies would be completely orphaned. Suddenly, her boycott on God no longer mattered. There was no one else who could help her.

Lord, help me. Please. Oh, please. Help.

Chief Paul Kennedy was driving back from a two-vehicle accident on the outskirts of LaMar

Pond when the dispatcher announced shots fired near his location. A young woman had called 911, screaming that her neighbor was shooting at her son's service coordinator and had taken off in his truck after her.

Paul switched on his siren and pushed the hands-free button to answer the call. "Chief Kennedy here. I'm less than a mile away, heading that direction now. Send backup."

Disconnecting as soon as she confirmed, he said a prayer for the safety of all involved. It was never pleasant to handle road rage. Adding a gun and winter weather into the mix could prove to be a disaster in the making.

He came around the curve, his headlights cutting through the dark. The snowflakes caught in the beams made him think of a snow globe. Then they hit a sight that chilled his heart.

A red SUV was stranded in a ditch. He knew that SUV. It belonged to Irene Martello, his best friend's younger sister. The girl whose trust he'd shattered so many years ago. She was also the widow of one of his officers, shot down on his watch. Three good reasons he'd never, ever want to see her in danger of any kind. But it looked like that was exactly what was happening.

Directly behind her car, he could see a dark pickup truck had pulled off and parked on the side of the road. And not to help. The driver, a large man with a fierce scowl on his bearded face, had opened his door. He had started to step out of the vehicle, a rifle in his bare hands. This man meant to harm Irene.

The moment Paul appeared, though, he halted. The bright lights and the loud wail of the siren made the bearded man jerk back into his truck before speeding off in the opposite direction. Paul wanted to chase him, needed to stop the maniac. But he needed to check on Irene more. Quickly, he called in a description of the truck and the driver, and called for an ambulance.

Parking his cruiser on the side of the road, he kept his lights on to warn any oncoming traffic to slow down. Then he strode to the driver's-side door. She was watching him, her face blood-less. From fear, or was she in shock? Either way, he sent up a silent prayer of thanks at the sight of her alive and alert. He rapped on the window. It wasn't necessary. She was already rolling it down.

"Irene? Are you okay?"

"Paul!" She choked out his name. For the first time in years, her gaze wasn't cool when she met his eyes. Fear and gratitude took pre-cedence over wounded pride. "I thought he was going to kill me!" Her voice wobbled slightly, but she wasn't crying. Anymore. The streaks left by earlier tears were evident.

He needed to calm her down, see if she was injured. "Easy, Irene. He's gone. Are you hurt anywhere? Anything broken?" He scanned her carefully.

She shook her head, then winced. His gaze narrowed in on her forehead. She wasn't bleeding. There was a dark shadow on her temple that concerned him. It could have been nothing, or a bruise forming. Hard to tell without proper lighting.

"Did you hit your head? It looks bruised. Any dizziness, or blurry vision?"

"I did bang it against the steering wheel when I went into the ditch. But I don't think I'm really hurt."

Hmm. He'd have her checked out when the ambulance arrived, just the same.

"What happened?" He kept his voice calm, even though he was feeling anything but.

"You know I started working at the Early Intervention program a couple of months ago?" He nodded. He remembered Jace saying something about that. "I was finishing a home visit. It was my last one of the day. When I first arrived, I accidentally went to the wrong house. That man answered the door and he was very angry to see me there. It was downright creepy.

Then, when I was leaving his neighbors after my visit, he came out of the house and started looking around. Not at me, but like he was searching for something. I started driving and he started running after me. I didn't wait, just took off. Then next thing I knew, I was waiting at the stop sign, and he came up behind me and boom—" she slapped a hand on her steering wheel "—he'd shot out my back window and was coming after me. He rammed his truck into me, twice. The road was icy, and I lost control. I really think he would have killed me if you hadn't arrived. How did you know I was in danger?"

He had to draw in three deep breaths before he could speak around the red haze threatening to overcome him. His normally calm demeanor was failing him as he tried to keep from thinking of what would have happened if he had been farther away. *Thank You, Lord, for placing me here in time to help.* Paul was a firm believer that the Lord was in charge.

"The family you'd visited with called nine-one-one. They were able to give the operator the address of the neighbor who attacked you. I was on my way there when I came across your vehicle. I need to check in and make sure an officer is on the scene. Then we can go from there."

She nodded, relaxing briefly in her seat. Only for a moment, though. Her eyes widened slightly and she sat ramrod straight in her seat, grimacing. Maybe she was more bruised than she'd let on. "There was a woman inside the house when I arrived. Young, nineteen, maybe twenty or twenty-one. I don't know what was going on in there, but she looked scared, Paul. Really scared."

"I'll get it checked out, Irene. I promise." Paul moved to the front of the car and thumbed the radio on his shoulder to get an update. When he was told that several officers were en route to the scene, he gave the order that they inform him immediately of any findings. He took one step back toward Irene, then stopped. Jace's shift would be ending soon. He'd want to know what had happened. Paul was his chief, but he was also his best friend. Jace should hear about it from him. Before he could change his mind, he reached back, pulled his cell phone from his pocket and dialed the familiar number.

"'Lo, Chief."

Paul winced, even though he'd expected him to answer. He loved Jace like a brother, and this would not be an easy conversation. Jace was used to dealing with violence, but telling him that the shooting target had been his sister this time was not going to go over well.

"Lieutenant Tucker." Paul hesitated. He always tried to keep things professional when they were at the station. They weren't at the station, however, and this was an unusual situation.

"Jace…" He addressed the man as a friend. "She's okay, but the woman shot at was Irene."

Silence. Then Jace's deep voice exploded over the phone.

"What? What happened? You're positive she's okay? Where are you?"

Paul gave him his location. "He rear-ended her, and her car went into a ditch. Her forehead looks bruised, but she seems lucid and aware. I'm sure she's fine, but I have an ambulance coming, just to be safe."

"She's not going to want to ride in an ambulance."

Didn't he know that? If he knew Irene, her first priority would be to get back to her kids as quickly as possible. Plus, she had never liked hospitals.

"Did you get the guy?" Jace's voice was calmer now.

"No. He ran off when he heard my siren. And I wasn't about to leave Irene on the side of the road, especially not knowing if she was injured or not."

"Appreciate that."

Paul moved back to the side of the car.

A distant siren rent the air. The ambulance. Finally. It was starting to snow harder, which would make the roads more treacherous. Before this night was done, there would be more than one accident for the crew to work on. He would feel much better knowing that Irene was taken care of.

"The ambulance is here now," Paul said to Jace. "Why don't you call your mom and let her know what's going on so she doesn't worry."

"How bad does Irene look?"

Bad? Paul nearly smiled. Irene never looked bad. Even bruised and shaken, the red-haired woman was perfect. Of course, he couldn't say that, although he had a suspicion that Jace was on to him.

"She looks fine. Maybe a little shaken." Blue eyes glared up at him. "Make that mad, will you?"

An unexpected chuckle floated down the line. "She's glaring at you, isn't she?"

"Sure is. And I much prefer that."

A pause. "Yeah. Me, too."

An angry Irene was much easier to deal with than a shaken or frightened one. He got that.

"Put her on, will you?"

Paul handed the phone to Irene, then moved away again to give her some privacy. When the ambulance crew came over, she returned the phone to him.

Paul gave them room to do their job. And he did his—setting up flares to warn oncoming traffic to take precautions. By the time he returned to the car, Irene was done being checked out. The paramedics were recommending a trip to the hospital to get her head checked out. As expected, she was set against going.

"You should go to the hospital to get checked out." Paul bent over for a closer look at the bruise. She rolled her eyes, making him grin.

Irene sighed. "I need to get home to my kids."

"I had Jace tell your mom where you were. He will make sure that they're taken care of. Besides, your car will need to be towed. There's no way you can drive it with the back window blown out. Go to the hospital, and we will bring your car back when it's drivable. If all it needs is a new windshield, that should be tomorrow morning."

He received another glare for his trouble. Why did it have to be this hard? He kept hoping that she would forgive him. Then again, what would he do if she did? It wasn't like he would be any good for a fine woman like Irene. He had way too much baggage. Too many other responsibilities around his neck.

A sudden noise caught his attention.

Irene started to speak. He raised his hand. When she started to look huffy, he said, "Wait. Do you hear something?"

Irene tilted her head, her curls brushing against her cheek as she did. He averted his gaze and was momentarily distracted by the fact that her left hand was ringless. He was sure she had still been wearing her wedding band last time he saw her.

There it was again. A scratching noise. And now a faint mewling sound. Coming from inside her SUV. Paul moved closer and leaned in. Irene backed away from him. Whether that was because he was too close or because it was him, he didn't know. And now was not the time to ponder it. If something was in Irene's car with her, he needed to get to the bottom of it, fast.

"Irene, I need you to do exactly what I say." He kept his voice at a low murmur, the epitome of calm and casual, even though his heart was beating fast.

For once, the stubborn woman nodded without arguing. Guess she was still pretty freaked-out. And who wouldn't be?

"Go get in my cruiser. I need to see what's in your car, but I don't want you here when I do. I need to focus on this completely."

He didn't say, *And your presence is already too distracting to me.* Although he could have. He surely could have.

Paul made eye contact with her, making sure she understood how important this was. She moved towards his car, wobbling slightly on the uneven road. He held on to her elbow until she was steady, then let her go. He watched as the female paramedic led her safely to his cruiser. The paramedics wouldn't leave the site of an accident until the patient either joined them in the ambulance or signed a refusing-treatment form. So at least, she wouldn't be alone and unguarded.

The moment he felt she was reasonably safe, Paul shined his flashlight into the back of the car. Nothing was there that he could see. But then he heard the mewling again. This time it was louder.

Moving to the back, he grabbed his gun in one hand and the light in the other. Bracing himself for a fight or to duck, he flashed his light in the back window—and nearly dropped the light in his shock.

Curled up on the floor of Irene's SUV was a small child. A little girl, although he was unsure of her age. No more than two, he guessed.

Judging by her dress and bonnet, she was Amish. She was shivering.

She was also covered in blood.

TWO

Paul pushed his gun back into the holster and yelled for the paramedics.

"I have a child here! Possibly injured."

He opened the door, stepping back to let it swing upward. The dome light came on, causing the little girl's eyes to squeeze shut. She whimpered and curled into a tighter ball. The poor little thing was scared to death. Who did she belong to? And how on earth had she gotten into the back of the car?

"It's okay, little one," he crooned softly. "I'm going to help you. What's your name?"

No response. She didn't even look up.

Paul heard shuffling feet, and the male paramedic stepped up beside him, only his eyes showing the level of his concern. In a job working with those who were injured or dangerous, you learned quickly to remain calm at all costs. That was the only way you survived. Paul knew from experience that bad things could happen when you didn't. When you lost control, who knew what sort of damage would result? When the man started to climb into the back of the SUV, the child drew back in terror.

"Let me." Sydney, the female paramedic, moved forward and climbed in, making soothing noises. The girl still pulled back, but her distress seemed to lessen. When Sydney moved toward her, the girl whimpered but was calm enough for the woman to examine her.

He felt someone at his side and knew without turning that Irene was there. Of course. Why would she do what he asked and remain in the car? After all, he was only the chief of police. It wasn't like he had any authority. Not with her, at any rate. Even if she didn't like him, she knew him too well to be intimidated by his authority.

"She has Down syndrome."

"What?" He looked at the little girl again.

"You see her eyes, and her face—I'm a special-education teacher, remember?" Irene's voice was hushed, soothing. A mother's voice. "Oh, she's beautiful. And so scared. Paul, is that blood on her dress?"

Sydney beat him to it. "Yes, but I don't think it's hers. I can't seem to find any visible bleeding injuries on her. But she is dehydrated. When she opened her mouth, her tongue was white and seemed dry. Her eyes seem a little sunken, too. I wouldn't rule out abuse, either. She needs to go to the hospital."

"How is it we didn't hear her before?"

Paul wanted to know that, too.

Sydney tilted her head. "My guess? She was either momentarily stunned or the noise from everything else drowned out the sound."

Paul had another thought, one that chilled him. "Or she's been conditioned to make no noise." Irene and both paramedics looked at him, startled. Maybe even a little confused. But he could see the dawning horror as the meaning of his words sank in.

"You mean she might have been punished for making any noise."

He nodded. "Yeah, that makes the most sense to me. Sorry to say."

Sydney moved to pick up the child. The little girl backed away, eyes flaring wild. The male paramedic—Trey?—tried to reach in and get her. Immediately, she went into a frenzy, shrieking and biting.

"Oh, hey, don't do that!"

Irene moved forward. Paul reached out a hand to caution her to stay back, then felt his own jaw drop when the child launched herself out of the car and into Irene's arms. Her little arms wound up about the woman's neck and clung tight. Almost strangling Irene. Her grip looked painful, but Irene didn't flinch. She held the child securely in her arms, murmuring comforting sounds. The child settled down.

"I guess I'm going to the hospital, after all." She smiled at the girl. Her eyes were sad. Paul could almost see her thinking. Some mother somewhere was missing her baby. Suddenly, her gaze flashed back up to Paul's. "Oh, my! I was in my client's house for almost an hour and I forgot to lock my car. When I got in, I didn't even look back there. Paul, I think that this baby was from that house, the one where the man who was shooting at me lives. I remember thinking I heard a child cry out when I was there."

Paul shook his head. Not in disagreement, but in horror. "I wouldn't be surprised if this sweet little thing was kidnapped and he was shooting to stop you from getting away with her once he realized she was gone. But now I have to see how she got there."

He stepped back to allow them to move past him to the ambulance.

"I need to call this in, see if we have any reports of missing children from the Amish community."

"Would Rebecca know?"

Sergeant Miles Olsen had recently gotten engaged, and his future wife's family was Amish. Rebecca had left the Amish community years ago before she was baptized, allowing her to keep her ties with her family. She was also deaf, and sometimes communication with her family broke down. "I'm not sure. Somehow, I doubt it. And I also need to check with the officers at the scene."

Paul returned to his car and made a call to the station. As he'd expected, there were no reports of any young Amish children vanishing in the area. Considering the discomfort most Amish felt at the idea of involving the police in their community problems, he wasn't surprised.

His next call should have been to child services. He hesitated. If there was someone willing to shoot Irene to keep the identity and location of this child secret, he didn't feel comfortable letting her stay with a regular foster family, who wouldn't have the means to protect themselves and the other children in their care. No, for the moment, this was still police business.

And that brought another concern to the front of his mind. Irene would be in the hospital, but when she left, would that man still be after her? Things obviously weren't on the up-and-up, and she had gotten a very clear view of him. Not to mention his house and the vehicles. Would he come after her again?

And what about that sweet little girl? He called the station again. Remembering the girl's reaction to Trey and himself, he asked for Sergeant Zerosky, fondly known as Sergeant Zee. She picked up, and he sent her over to the hospital to keep watch. He knew she'd protect both Irene and the child.

He pushed the button on his radio again to speak with the officers on the scene.

"There wasn't much to find where the shooting happened. Some glass. Tire marks," Sergeant Gavin Jackson reported. "We're back at the house where the shooter lived. It's a mess. And Olsen found blood on the floor of the back bedroom. I can't tell how recent. It's dry. It's gonna take us a while longer to process this scene."

"Okay, this is a possible kidnapping, and maybe even a murder case. I have a child in custody, presumably kept in that house, who was then stashed away in a vehicle. She's on her way to the hospital right now. While you're processing the scene, keep your eyes peeled for anything that might help us to identify a small Amish girl. Oh, and Irene says she probably has Down syndrome."

"Irene? Jace's sister?"

"Yeah. She was visiting a nearby home. And the child was in her car when she came out—not that Irene noticed at the time, with that maniac chasing after her. We just found the kid about twenty minutes ago. Listen, someone will have to interview the neighbors, too. See what they know about the people at that house."

"Sure thing, boss. I'll keep ya posted."

Paul disconnected. He sat for a minute, musing about the sequences of events. He liked to be able to envision things in his head in order to understand how all the loose pieces fit together.

By the time the tow truck had arrived and pulled the SUV out of the ditch, Jace had appeared. He parked his cruiser behind Paul's, but kept his lights on. Jace stepped out of his vehicle, then sauntered over to meet Paul, looking like a man without a care in the world. Paul knew better. He could see the tense set of Jace's shoulders.

"Hey, Paul." Jace stopped beside him, his eyes grim as he watched his sister's SUV being towed away, a jagged hole where the back window should have been. "I'm going to go to the hospital to see my sister, then I will drive her back to my mom's house. She's got Reenie's kids."

Paul smiled. Only Jace could get away with calling Irene "Reenie."

"She's fine. She had been starting to refuse treatment—against my better judgment—when we made a little discovery."

Jace whistled after Paul had finished bringing him up-to-date. "Whoever said life in a small town was dull? And we have no idea where this child came from?"

"None. It's a mystery. I do want to head to the hospital to get a report on the child's condition." And on Irene's.

Paul drove back toward LaMar Pond. The struggle not to speed was causing his leg to ache with tension. The last thing he needed was to cause another accident on this snowy night, but he was so concerned about Irene that his nerves were taut.

She'd had more than her share of pain in her life. And she might not like it, but if she was in danger, then she'd just have to get used to having him around until she was safe again.

He wouldn't take no for an answer.

What kind of person could take another woman's baby? Irene's heart was shattered as she struggled to withhold the tears brought on by the child's fear and sorrow. It wasn't a hard jump to imagine a mother somewhere, suffering through a nightmare.

Irene held the little girl close as the doctor examined her. She knew the doctor was annoyed that she was getting in his way. She could hear it in his fussy voice and see it as he peered over the tops of his glasses at her. At them. But it made no difference. She had tried to set the child down. The doctors and nurses had tried to coax her away from Irene.

It was no use. The child fought and kicked out any time someone tried to take her from her chosen protector. Which was how it came to be that Irene was allowed to hold her while the doctor examined her. And it was she who had helped the child out of her bloodstained dress. The process was made difficult because the girl wouldn't completely release Irene. Eventually, it was managed. Irene was out of breath by that time.

"Well, the good news is that the child doesn't appear to be hurt. She needs some nutritious food, a bath and, I expect, rest."

Irene nodded. She had already surmised all that. "But the blood? Is any of it hers?"

Please say no.

"No."

She sagged slightly with relief, then caught herself and forced her tired back to straighten. She couldn't give in to the weariness that was dragging at her.

Someone knocked on the door. The child

snuggled in closer. Irene leaned down and kissed the child's head, offering what comfort she could. The door opened and Paul peeked into the room. Some of the familiar annoyance surged up briefly. Then it faded, when she remembered how happy she'd been to see him earlier. There had been a time when she had dreamed of Paul noticing her, back when they were both teenagers. Then he *had* noticed her, and for a few short months, she'd been happier than she'd ever been. Until he'd broken her trust and wounded her young heart.

She'd been devastated.

She'd managed to get over that. Had told herself she was better off without him. He'd hung out with a rough crowd back then, she mused. Well, except for Jace. She'd been sure Paul would end up arrested or worse. Before that could happen, he'd moved away for a few years. She couldn't believe it when Jace said he'd become a cop.

Not that she'd cared. She had fallen in love, gotten married and started a family. And then he had come back and become Tony's boss. She had resented that, at first. After all, Tony had seniority. But Tony took it in stride, and, as time went on, Paul had proved to be a good boss. The reckless kid she'd known had learned to control his wild side and become dedicated to serving others. He'd also apparently developed a strong relationship with God.

She had held on to her doubt, waiting for him to disappoint her again.

But tonight, he had been a real gift. If he hadn't come around that corner when he had, she would be dead. And who knew what would have happened to the little girl?

"Hey," he said in a loud whisper. "Jace will be here in a minute. He's talking with your mom on the phone." He indicated the little girl with a nod. "How is she?"

"Well, she's not injured," the doctor replied. "Is someone from child services coming for her?"

Irene grimaced. She had known that would be the next question, and she didn't like it. Not that she had anything against child services. They did a job very few people had the stomach for. But she knew that her new friend was not going to go willingly.

"I have not called child services yet," Paul responded, his voice deep and sure.

What? Shocked, her gaze flew in his direction.

He met her eyes and shrugged. "As far as I'm concerned, this is still a police matter. Speaking of which, Doc, I will need her clothes with blood for DNA testing."

"I'll ask my nurse. Mary—"

All conversation stopped as the girl's head whipped around.

"Does she recognize the name, do you think?" Irene looked between the two men. They looked as surprised as she felt. "Maybe it's her name."

Leaning back so she could see the small face, Irene tested her theory. "Mary? Hi, Mary."

The smile she received was like a ray of sunshine. Mary giggled and hunched her shoulders. It may or may not have been affirmative, but it was better than calling her "the child."

"Okay, then. We will need to keep Mary with us for the time being."

At the name, Mary smiled at Paul. He blinked. An answering smile softened the edges of his mouth. When was the last time she had seen a tender smile on his face? Paul was always in total control of himself. Her heart fluttered as the memory of that same smile from her high school days floated up to the forefront of her mind.

Not going there. He had broken her trust and her faith before. She may have forgiven him, had even allowed his presence in her life and that of her children's due to his friendship with Jace and Tony, but no more. And even if she was willing to believe he could be relied on, if there was one thing she didn't need, it was an emotional entanglement with another cop.

"Where will she stay?"

Paul scratched the top of his head. She knew that mannerism. He was still trying to figure things out. To make all the pieces fit.

"I don't know." She smiled at the admission. She had known it. "I was thinking of having a protective detail with Sergeant Zee in charge. Thought Mary would be more at ease with a woman in charge."

Irene nodded, saddened. A protective detail made sense, but it was a shame that it was needed. This little girl should be with her mother. Hopefully, Mary would be reunited with her family soon.

Jace arrived. Without a word, he walked over and leaned in to kiss Irene's forehead, careful not to crush Mary, who had fallen asleep. Irene blinked at the sweet gesture. She understood. Years ago, their baby sister Ellie had been killed. This night had reminded them all of their mortality.

The only good thing was that Mary slept through the transfer as Irene passed her off to the nurse who would finish cleaning up the child before turning her over to the police. Irene knew Sergeant Zee. The woman was competent and kind. She had also been a caretaker for her grandmother for a while. She would take good care of Mary.

If Mary let her.

Well, that wasn't Irene's problem. She tried to keep her mind from focusing on the little girl.

"Irene."

Oh, yeah. Paul.

She turned, lifting an eyebrow in question. In place of his normal unruffled demeanor, his brow was furrowed. He was a troubled man.

"I may need you to come in and look at the files to see if you recognize the man who attacked you if no one else can. I will check with his neighbors first. If we can't identify him, I will need to schedule an appointment with the forensic artist to come up with a good sketch we can pass around."

"Okay. I can stop by the station tomorrow, if you need me to."

Jace interrupted, "We won't be able to have anyone work with the artist until next week. You remember? Tara had surgery and won't be back until then."

Paul's mouth twisted. "I had forgotten. Well, if all works out, he'll be someone already in our database. Wouldn't that make life easier?"

Neither responded. Nor did he seem to expect a response.

"Come on, sis. I'll drive you home."

Irene started to head out with her brother. Then she stopped and turned to find Paul's deep brown eyes trained on her. His short dark hair was practically standing on end in places. He'd been running his hands through it. This had been a stressful evening for all of them.

"Paul? Thank you. I mean it. You saved my life tonight."

He nodded and flashed her a weary smile. "Anytime, Irene. I'm glad I was in the area."

Feeling they'd said everything that needed to be said, she left the room. She was so worn-out that she closed her eyes the moment she was seated in the passenger seat of Jace's cruiser.

All she wanted to do was go in and hug her boys. She needed to reassure herself that they were safe and happy. The image of little Mary with her bloodstained clothing was burned into her brain. She would remember that sight for the rest of her life.

At her mother's house, she marched quickly up the walk and in through the front door. Jace had obviously salted the sidewalk and steps, she was happy to note. Her mom met her in the kitchen. Irene endured her mother's scrutiny with as much patience as she could gather. Her mother needed the same reassurance she did.

"Mom, where are the boys?"

"They're watching a Christmas movie." Melanie Tucker, Jace's wife, moved into the kitchen, holding her year-old daughter, Ellie, in her arms.

Irene let the tension roll off her shoulders. She was safe. They were safe. She stepped past her sister-in-law, running a finger down her niece's cheek.

In the living room, she heard the soft voices of her children. A sudden rush of tears caught her off guard. She struggled for control. They had almost lost her. If Paul Kennedy had been farther away, this night might have had a whole different ending. For the first time in a long time, she felt as if she was being watched over. She shrugged the feeling off.

And thought again of that little girl, left alone. What would become of her?

Then another thought struck. Would the man be able to find out who she was? He'd seen her at the neighbor's house. She had been carrying a bag with the Early Intervention logo on it.

Irene hugged her arms close to her. Would he come looking for her?

The day had started with so much hope. Now it was turning into a nightmare. As long as that man stayed at large, she didn't know how she would ever feel that she and her children were safe.

THREE

"Chief, you need to come out here."

Paul shifted so his phone was wedged between his shoulder and his chin as he shrugged back into his coat. Sergeant Olsen's voice was slightly muffled, but he could still hear the words clearly. Jerking his shoulder to adjust the fit of the coat, he took the cell phone back in his hand and strode out the sliding doors and back into the cold, snowy night.

"I'm heading out now, Olsen. Just needed to wait for Sergeant Zee to get here." He felt a little guilty. She had no idea what was coming when Mary woke up. Maybe it would be fine and Mary would take to her the way she had to Irene. Maybe. But, somehow, he doubted it.

Thinking of Irene left a hollow feeling in his stomach. Was she safe? Jace would have called if something more had happened. But he couldn't get the image of the bearded man out of his mind. He didn't look like a man who would give up. One thing was sure—Paul wouldn't be able to focus as long as Irene was still in danger. He grabbed his phone and put in a call, directing that someone would drive past her house each hour. Being the chief of police definitely had its perks.

At the scene, he parked his cruiser in the driveway behind Olsen's vehicle. It was obvious that the driveway had not been plowed in the past few hours. He couldn't really tell if he was on the pavement or on the grass. Not that it mattered.

"Chief." Olsen trudged through the snow to meet him. "Jackson is with the neighbors right now. The people who called nine-one-one. I figured you might want to go over. And then there are some things in the house I want your opinion on."

Paul nodded. "Right. I'll head right over." He lifted his gaze to the house. It looked dark and ghoulish at night, very poorly lit. It had obviously not been kept up. Just what horrors did it hide inside? The sooner they finished processing this scene, the easier he would feel.

Sergeant Jackson was still talking to the family when Paul entered the room.

"Sir, this is Mr. and Mrs. Zilcher. They called in the shots when the man started shooting after Irene. I mean, Mrs. Martello."

Paul focused in on the stressed faces of the young couple. What a way to spend their evening.

"Folks, thanks for calling it in. Mrs. Martello is safe, no doubt because you were so brave." That was certainly true. He shuddered to think what would have happened if the couple hadn't notified the police. He wouldn't have known to head in this direction, and Irene...

He took in a deep breath, noticing that everyone was staring at him. Now was not the time to think of Irene. Pushing thoughts of the lovely widow out of his mind, he recommitted himself to getting to the bottom of the case. As soon as humanly possible. With lots of Divine help.

Lord, I place Irene, my officers, that child, and all involved in Your hands.

"Do you know the people who live in that house?"

Mrs. Zilcher bit her lip, then she ducked her head, as if ashamed. "I know it sounds bad, but we avoided them. They seemed, I don't know... Honey?"

She turned to her husband.

"The first time we saw them, the younger man—not the one who fired the shots—yelled at our older son for playing too near their property. Now, Joel is only six. He wasn't doing any harm, but that man scared him so much that ever since, we have just avoided them at all costs."

Paul nodded. It made sense. "And would I be correct to assume that your son never went near the house again?"

"Chief, this has always been a very safe area. But in the past two months since they arrived, I don't even let him go outside in the backyard alone. And it's fenced in."

Smart move.

"What about this afternoon? After the man pursued Mrs. Martello, did he come back?"

"No. But within half an hour, all of them took off." Mrs. Zilcher twisted her wedding ring. "I didn't see them come out, but I heard lots of loud revving, and then the truck and the car both left. I haven't seen them since."

The man who went after Irene must have warned them when he saw Paul's police car approaching.

Paul broke into their narrative. "Who is 'them'? Can you describe the people you saw there? Anything you can remember will help. Age, gender, descriptions…anything at all."

"Well, let's see," Mrs. Zilcher ticked them off on her fingers. "There was that young guy. Just an average-looking man. Maybe in his early twenties? Blondish hair, collar length. Average build. Really, no one you'd look twice at if you saw him on the street or at the store. Then the big guy who shot at Irene, our service co-ordinator. He was a handsome enough man. Well groomed. But he looked so fierce. Probably late thirties, early forties. Not overweight, but big. Definitely over six feet. The last guy I never got a real good look at." She turned to her husband.

He shook his head. "I didn't, either. He was usually pretty covered up. Hats, hooded sweatshirts, hunting coats. Got the impression that he tried to keep from being noticed. Only glimpsed him briefly when I did see him. And then I only really saw him from the back."

"Did you ever notice a young woman, maybe in her late teens or early twenties, at the house?"

Both of them shook their heads.

So how long had she been there? And was she one of them or another victim? Paul was starting to get a very ugly picture in his mind.

"What about any children?"

"Children?" Mrs. Zilcher blinked, startled. "No, I certainly never saw any children there."

Half an hour later, that picture was even darker.

Going through the abandoned house was not something that Paul was likely to forget. In the back bedroom, around where Irene would have seen the girl looking out the window, there was indeed dried blood on the floor. Recent blood. There was some on the wall, too. One spot looked like a handprint, tiny and low to the ground. Either from a very young person or someone who was very small. The team had already pulled fingerprints and would see if they could track down any matches. Hopefully, there would be something in their system that would connect to either Mary or the girl Irene had seen. Paul refused to think of what might have happened to her. She was gone, so there was a shot she was still alive, though his faith in finding her alive was fading. And it would continue to fade every hour that they couldn't find her.

His cell phone rang. It was Irene. His pulse spiked. Irene never called him.

"Irene? Are you okay? Is someone hurt?"

There was a moment of silence on the other end, then a breathy sound, almost a laugh but not quite. "Paul, I'm fine. You startled me. I'm not used to hearing you yell."

He *had* yelled, hadn't he? Stretching his neck to the side to relieve his sudden tension, he tried again, keeping his voice calm.

"Sorry. I didn't mean to yell. But you caught me at a tense moment."

"Oh. Is everything okay?" Her voice was reluctantly concerned.

"With me, everything's dandy. But this house, Irene, it's bad. Really bad." He shook his head, deciding not to say any more. She might have been married to a cop, but she still was a civilian. And he wanted to spare her from the rougher parts of his job. Not that she'd ever give him a chance to share anything more. He had more or less shattered any chance with her, now or in the future, when he'd abandoned her on that long-ago homecoming night. If only he could explain why...

He scoffed silently. That would make her even more resistant, knowing his secrets. No, his secret scars would have to remain that way.

"I just realized something, that's why I called. When I was thinking about the girl in the house, the one who was watching me? Well, I just realized that she looked like there was something around her neck. And now, thinking about it, I believe they were bonnet straps. I think she was Amish, too, just like Mary."

"What else was she wearing?"

"I couldn't tell. She was mostly out of view. I'm sorry. I'm probably not much help." Her voice was growing embarrassed.

"No, actually, you are. I have more information than I did before—that's always a good thing."

So now they needed to search for a missing child and a missing girl. They would start searching in the local Amish communities. If they didn't succeed there, then they would widen their search.

"Thanks, Irene. I mean it. Every detail helps."

"How's Mary doing?"

His heart softened. Irene, always thinking about the plight of others. She'd always been that way. "I left her with Sergeant Zee."

"Did she go quietly?"

"Yeah, but that was probably because she was asleep."

"Paul!"

He sighed, rolling his eyes. She couldn't see him, after all. "I will check on her first thing in the morning. Promise."

After disconnecting the call, he went to the room where Olsen was taking pictures.

"What did you want to see me about, Olsen?"

"Look at all this stuff, Chief. What do you make of it?"

There was a trunk full of children's clothes in various sizes and colors. All of them showed signs of wear. And there was a pair of Amish breeches on top. Beside the trunk, there was a bottle, still half-full, and a dirty sippy cup.

"Mary wasn't the only child these people have taken, is my guess. Maybe they still have one or two of them. What they were planning to do with them, I don't know. But we need to find them. Fast."

Before any more children were taken. Or worse.

Irene couldn't remember the last time she'd been so tired. Last night, she had tossed and turned. When she had finally fallen into a restless sleep, it was to be disturbed in her dreams by images of being chased at gunpoint. She finally gave up. It was only quarter after six, but she knew trying to fall back to sleep was hopeless. Throwing back the covers, she padded to the boys' bedroom and peeked in. Both were still sound asleep. She sighed, aching with tenderness at the sight of the peaceful children.

Since the peace wouldn't last, she might as well get ready for the day. She dressed in casual jeans and an emerald green turtleneck sweater. She lugged out her workbag, shaking off the memories.

Pulling out her laptop, she spent some time finishing an evaluation report. By the time it was completed, she could hear the boys arguing in the kitchen. They were up early. Normally, the thought of facing their fighting at seven o'clock on a Saturday morning would annoy her. The memory of the night before washed away any trace of aggravation. She was here, safe, with her kids. That was a lot to be grateful for.

She entered the kitchen, kissed her boys and ruffled their hair as she walked past. Their dog, Izzy, was peacefully snoozing under the table.

"Hi, Mommy!" Matthew peeked up at her with his ragged grin, his front teeth missing. "Can we have waffles for breakfast?"

That was Matthew. His stomach always came first.

"Waffles sound good to me. AJ?"

Her older son peered at her through his new glasses. My, he was looking so grown-up. When had her baby become such a big boy?

Tony would have loved this.

"Waffles are yummy. Can we set up the tree today?"

Ugh. The Christmas tree. One more thing she didn't want to face. But at least she could give her children the fun parts of Christmas.

She made them waffles, and then the boys helped her drag out the artificial tree and ornaments. She sat down in the center of the living room floor to sort the ornaments, AJ by her side. As she was unraveling the lights, Matthew stood at the window, his face intent. She frowned when she noted him standing on his tiptoes, straining to see something.

"Matthew, why are you staring out the window?"

"I'm watching the man, Mommy."

She set aside the strand of lights in her hands, unease dancing down her spine. It could be nothing, but she wasn't taking any chances.

"What man, darling?" *Calm. Stay calm. The last thing they need is for you to overreact.*

"That man across the street." Matthew hadn't turned around, still intent on the stranger.

"Matthew, come away from the window." How she was able to keep from raising her voice she'd never know.

Something in her tone must have said she meant business, though, because Matthew left his place and skittered down on the floor beside her, his small face pale. The freckles on his cheeks stood out.

"Mommy, I'm scared."

Her poor baby.

"It's okay, love, I'm going to call Chief Paul. He'll know what to do."

Crawling over to the end table, she grabbed her phone and dialed Paul's number with shaking fingers. It wasn't until the phone started ringing that she wondered why she'd instinctively called him and not Jace. Because Paul helped her last night? Of course that was why. She moved to the window and peered out, taking care to keep out of sight. There parked on the street across from her was a dark sedan. Was that the one that had been sitting at the bearded man's house?

"Hello."

Paul's deep drawl sent a shiver down her spine. She scolded herself. She didn't have time for that. Sure, he was strong and was well respected in LaMar Pond, but he was hiding something. She was certain. Only, right now, it didn't seem to matter.

"Paul," she whispered. "There's a man sitting in his car outside my house. He's watching us. And I can't be sure, but it may be one of the people from that house. The car looks familiar."

"Irene, are the boys with you?" His voice had lost all trace of the lazy, relaxed drawl. Its intensity communicated his concern over the phone.

"Yes, we are all here."

"Okay, this is what I want you to do. Make sure the doors are locked. And keep away from the windows. Whatever you do, do *not* answer the door unless it's me or Jace. I'm going to call him right now. He's closer to your house. I will be over as soon as I can."

Click.

She slid the phone back into her pocket and looked at the two frightened faces before her.

"Boys, let's go back to the kitchen."

"Aren't we setting up the tree?" AJ asked, disappointment on his face.

Matthew didn't argue. He was already halfway there.

"We'll make Christmas cookies first," Irene declared, coming up with an impromptu diversion. Both faces brightened.

Her phone rang again. Paul.

"Jace is on his way, too. Sit tight, Irene. We'll be there ASAP."

Her nerves were shot by the time Jace arrived. She saw his car pull around the corner from the kitchen window. Immediately, an engine revved. She heard tires squeal as a car raced in the opposite direction. The watcher had left. The cruiser's lights burst into a swirl of blue and red as Jace followed in pursuit.

Less than five minutes later, someone pounded on her front door. Yelping, she dropped the bowl of icing she'd just whipped together. The silver bowl bounced, flinging white icing on the cupboard doors and all over her blue jeans.

"Irene? It's me. Paul."

Paul. She placed a hand over her pounding

heart and closed her eyes, fighting the urge to wilt against the countertops.

"Mommy, Chief Paul is here." AJ frowned as the chief called out again. "Should I let him in?"

"No! No, I will do it. You boys stay here and wipe up this mess. Please."

They looked less than thrilled, but both nodded. She had expected some protest. Especially from AJ. That neither boy offered even a token resistance told her that they had sensed the seriousness of the situation.

She moved to the door and opened it. She came face-to-face with Paul, his hand raised to knock again. Patent relief flashed across his face as he saw her. His gaze moved over her, checking for injury or signs of distress. She knew the moment he spotted the icing by the way his mouth curled up at the sides. Not exactly a grin, but she could tell he was amused.

Only for a moment, however. The smile vanished so fast she might have imagined it.

"Jace went after the guy," she informed him.

He nodded. "Yeah, he almost caught him, too. The guy got out and took off running across the interstate. Unfortunately, Jace didn't get a good look at him. The Zilchers are coming in to look through the data files. I think you should do that, too. Immediately, if not sooner. In the meantime, Jace is going to go over the car the guy abandoned. See what he can get from it."

There was no way she could refuse. If this was related to what had happened the day before, they had found out where she lived. The situation was as serious and urgent as it could get. "My kids..."

Paul laid a hand on her shoulder. She shivered. The warmth of his hand spread out. Not now. This was not a good idea. She moved back.

"Take them to your mom's house. Jace already called her."

She had no choice. Reluctantly, she agreed. The reluctance was partially because she didn't want to be separated from them right now. And, she admitted to herself, partly because she didn't like this awareness of Paul that seemed to be returning. The thought of spending more time alone with him was unsettling. She wasn't a high school girl anymore—what was wrong with her?

As she bundled them up for the trip to her mother's, she couldn't stop the dread quivering in her belly. She had to work hard to keep her apprehension from showing on her face. Kids were sensitive. They would pick up on her disquiet in a heartbeat.

But her mother's heart wouldn't let it go.

"Paul," she began as she made her way back to the living room with two boys wrapped up tight in their winter gear. She stopped. Paul was no longer alone. Jace and Miles were there, deep in conversation. The men stopped talking when she appeared.

Paul nodded at the other two men and approached Irene and the boys. "Hey, guys. How would you like a ride to your grandma's in a police car?" He grinned at the boys like he was suggesting an adventure, rather than moving to get them out of harm's way. "Sergeant Olsen was wanting to visit your gran. Think she'll have cookies he can swipe?"

AJ nodded, his face serious. "Yeah, Granny always has cookies. But he better ask first."

"And say please," Matthew added.

"I'm sure he will." Paul patted their heads affectionately.

His eyes, though, when he glanced back at Irene, were completely devoid of humor.

He's as worried as I am.

That scared her most of all.

FOUR

Two hours later, she sat back with a sigh, disappointed. No one in the mug shots looked familiar. But she really hadn't expected they would. Jace was more fortunate. Mrs. Zilcher had identified the owner of the car. Jace felt certain it was the same man who had escaped from him that morning. His runner was wanted for several assault charges. A man by the name of Niko Carter. Jace immediately put out the alert to apprehend the young man. Unfortunately, the car was clean of any evidence that could be connected to Mary or other missing children.

There was nothing left for her to do here.

"I guess I should get the boys and go back home," she said to no one in particular. "I don't have my car back yet. I'm going to need a ride."

Jace stood and stretched. "I can drive you. Just give me a few minutes."

Paul's voice stopped him. "It's okay, Jace. I

want to talk with Irene about what we should do to keep her and the boys safe. I'll take her to your mom's. It would be more efficient."

Jace acquiesced, his lips twitching as he raised an eyebrow. Irene felt her skin warm as embarrassment—and something she wasn't quite ready to name—sizzled under her skin. As she walked out past Jace, she gave him her best narrow-eyed stare, daring him to tease. He shrugged, but continued to smile. Then he surprised her by standing and kissing her cheek. Jace might not have said it, but she knew he was concerned about her. After their sister Ellie had died, Jace had become overprotective of Irene. It had taken years for him to learn to let her have her space, but she knew it still ate at him to see her distressed or in any kind of danger. She reached out and squeezed his arm, silently telling him she understood.

Once she was seated beside him and they were on their way, Paul didn't waste any time bringing up his concerns.

"Irene." His deep voice settled between them.

She turned her head and raised an eyebrow.

"I talked with Zee while you were looking at the files. Mary's doing fine, although she's a little cranky."

"That's good to hear. Thank you for telling me."

He nodded, then continued. "I don't need to tell you that this is a potentially dangerous situation. I'm changing my orders. Instead of an hourly drive-by, I'm putting a detail on your house around the clock. Just until the danger passes."

She'd been expecting that, and as much as she treasured her independence, she accepted it gratefully. It wasn't only her life at stake here. Her boys were in danger, too.

"The department's going to be stretched tight between the detail on you and searching for Mary's family."

She nodded. Then a thought occurred to her. "What about my car?"

"I will check on the status when we arrive at your mother's house."

The boys were thrilled to see her arrive with Paul. They chattered happily about the time spent with their grandmother and the new puppies her neighbor's dog had just had that morning. Irene fended off subtle hints about getting a new puppy with ease born of practice. She could hear Paul talking to the mechanic about her car in the other room.

"Your vehicle's fixed," he announced as he entered the room. "The only problem was the windshield, and your insurance covered that.

We'll drive by and pick it up on our way back to your house."

She smiled. It would be nice to have her car back. She thanked her mother, then gathered her boys and got them situated in the cruiser. Twenty minutes later, they had stopped to get her SUV, and were again on their way. It was comforting to look back in her review mirror and see Paul following her.

The closer they drove to her home, however, the more anxiety twisted in her gut. Would that man be watching the house again when they returned? Would she and her children be safe? She breathed a sigh of relief when she rounded the corner and no one was there. Still, she waited until Paul was parked behind her to get out of the car.

She scooted the kids inside as soon as Paul had checked the house and declared it was safe. When they looked like they wanted to complain, she reminded them that Izzy had probably been lonely and would need to be fed and walked. They hurried inside to see to the dog.

She nodded her thanks at Paul, then continued into the house. Paul pulled out his phone. She could hear his voice murmuring as she closed the door before moving into the kitchen.

Should she have stayed at her mother's house for a day or two? She pondered the idea for a brief moment before rejecting it. No. Her mom was a worrier. And she still had normal things to do. Like go to work. And the boys had to go to school. She'd have to consider her next step carefully.

She put a kettle on the stove. A cup of tea might help settle her nerves a bit. Paul walked into the room just as she began pouring hot water over the mixed-berry tea bag.

She indicated the tea with her free hand. "Want a cup? Or I can make some coffee."

A smile flickered briefly across his handsome face. "Nah. I'm good. Listen, we might have a slight problem."

She tensed. Apprehension skittered up her spine. What else could go wrong?

"I have a small gap in the morning where I will be without coverage for you. Jace and Miles are flying out tonight because they are witnesses in a trial this coming week. Sergeant Zee's looking after Mary. I have Thompson keeping an eye on her house. And the other officers have assignments they're working on. I'm the only one left, and I take my mother to church every week. She can't drive anymore. Her vision's too bad now."

Church. Did he expect her to go with him? She hadn't gone inside a church since Tony had died unless it was for a wedding. Lifting her mug, she took a small sip, holding the hot liquid in her mouth to enjoy the subtle flavors.

Apparently, her ambivalence got through to him. Paul's expression was bland, but she could feel his withdrawal. "Of course, my mom will understand if I cancel one week. She can watch services on TV."

And now she felt mean.

"We'll go with you." What was she thinking? But it was too late to back down. "The boys and I will go with you and your mother to church."

Maybe, with all that was going on, maybe it was time she gave God another chance. Paul's expression lightened. It almost made up for the mass of nerves in her stomach. Almost.

Paul hung around until the first patrol showed up outside the house. She could see the officer inside the car. It was one of the older officers she'd known for years, and the sight of him was comforting.

The day passed smoothly, but by nighttime, her nerves were all jangled. The phone rang. She let out a shriek, startled by the noise.

Silly, she chastised herself.

"Hello?" she answered the phone.

Whoever it was hung up.

Wrong number. Or was it him? Had he called to see if she was home? Running to the living room, she stood beside the window and peered out. The current patrol was there. She could see the man inside the car moving around. She was safe.

An hour later, the phone rang again.

Again, the person on the other end of the line hung up.

Now she was freaked-out. Maybe she should run out and tell the cop. Tell him what? That someone had hung up on her? That was hardly a crime. And there was no way on earth she was walking outside and leaving her babies inside unprotected. They were in bed, but they would still be vulnerable.

No. She would wait.

After changing into sweats, she tried to sleep. She tossed and turned until, finally, she dropped off into a restless sleep.

Only to be awoken by the sound of the dog barking at five in the morning. Not just barking. But growling and lunging at the back door.

Irene jumped out of bed, her heart pounding. Running to the boys' room, she checked to make sure they were safe. Both were sound asleep.

Izzy continued to bark. Irene crept down the hall in time to see the dog lunge viciously at the back door, scratching the wood as she tried to get at whatever was threatening the family.

Izzy never did that. She had been too well trained.

That's when Irene knew. Something evil was out there. Or someone.

What was that noise? Paul had been feeling a bit sleepy after sitting in the dark for the past two hours, but now he was on full alert. There. He heard it again. From where he sat inside his cruiser in Irene's driveway, it sounded like it was coming from inside her house, though he couldn't tell from where.

Paul rolled down his window and listened.

Izzy was barking. And it wasn't a normal bark. It was the bark of a dog protecting her family. Adrenaline flooded his system. Irene and the boys might be in danger. He reached over and picked up the flashlight, shoving it in his pocket as he hopped out of his vehicle and ran up to her front door, mindful of the snow crunching beneath his feet. He would be of no use to her if he fell and injured himself on her driveway.

He pounded on her door.

She screamed from inside the house. His heart stopped at the sound.

"Irene!" He raised his hand to pound on the door a second time.

Footsteps, running toward him. Then the

door was yanked open. He saw her white face for just a moment before she launched herself into his arms. Unprepared for the onslaught, he stumbled back two steps until he regained his balance. He hugged her and, at the same time, moved them both inside the house. Shutting the door, he gave her a squeeze, then released her. The dog was still growling at the back door.

"Are you and the boys all right?"

She opened her mouth, but only a broken sob emerged. All she could manage was a nod. That was fine. As long as she and the kids were unhurt. That was all that mattered.

"Mommy? Mommy!" AJ and Matthew hurtled into the room, tears on their cheeks. Nothing scared a child as much as knowing their parent was frightened. Irene visibly pulled her emotions under control.

Izzy was still barking at the back door, scratching frantically to get out.

"It's okay, boys. When Izzy started barking, Paul came to check on us. The noise of him knocking startled me, that's all." She bent and kissed the boys. They didn't look convinced, but allowed her to lead them back to their bedroom. Paul took advantage of her absence and checked the locks on the doors and the windows, nodding in satisfaction when all was secure. She returned to stand near him.

He absolutely should not be noticing the scent of her shampoo as she stood close. Moving to the door, he refocused on the job at hand. Irene pulled the dog back from the door.

"You stay here," Paul commanded, pulling the flashlight out of his pocket. He flipped it on, keeping the beam low. His service weapon was in his other hand. "Lock the door after me. Don't open it until I tell you to. No matter what."

The moment she nodded, he was out the door. He waited just a moment until he heard it latch and the dead bolt was slid back in place. Then he was off, searching for any sign of movement or disturbance. The snow was far too messed up by footprints from the Martello family and Izzy to really see if any new tracks were visible.

As he approached the backyard, he noticed that the barking inside the house had lessened. Then it stopped altogether. He sighed. Whoever or whatever had been there had likely taken off again. Who knows? Maybe it wasn't a person at all, but a black bear, instead. They sometimes woke up and left their dens, wandering around searching for more food. It wouldn't be the first time a confused bear had wandered so close to a home.

It was a possible explanation—but not a very likely one. He didn't buy it for a second. And a minute later, his gut was proved correct as he moved along the thick row of bushes that lined the perimeter of the property line. Near the north corner, he found a suspicious break in the shrubbery. A hole just large enough for someone to slip through. Moving closer, he shined his light on the ground. There, showing up starkly on the white snow, were cut branches. No bear had done this. The branches were sawed cleanly off. Likely with a pair of heavy-duty shears. So whoever had done it had come prepared. Which meant that Irene was being watched by someone who knew there was a policeman parked out front and had taken steps to sneak in through the back. He used his radio to call in to the station. Ryan Parker and Gavin Jackson were on duty.

"Chief?"

Jackson. Concisely, Paul brought the officer up to speed on what he'd found.

"Okay. Parker and I will be out ASAP."

Paul hung up and looked again at the bush. Someone was very determined.

He shuddered. What would have happened if Irene hadn't had Izzy to warn him of the would-be intruder?

Stop. He couldn't let himself go there. Nor could he allow any of the emotional attachments he had for the family, or for Irene, to interfere with his focus. It was on him to keep Irene, AJ and Matthew safe. He would do everything in his power to protect them. Which meant putting the people out to get Irene behind bars.

If he could protect Irene and her family and get little Mary back to her family, he would be content.

He remembered the look on Irene's face when they'd found the little girl. It had been plain to see that her heart ached for the child's parents. Just thinking of Irene made him anxious to check on her again, make sure she was still all right.

"Irene?" Paul called, knocking. "Open up. It's me, Paul."

Subdued and worn-out, she let him in. It had only been a day and a half since this whole mess started, and yet it seemed to have aged her right before his eyes. How much could one person take?

Paul shut the door behind him, locked it, then faced her. His eyes narrowed as they took in her expression. Without a word, he reached out and enfolded her into his embrace. She let him. Which proved just how unsettled she was. After a minute, he felt her stiffen and pull back. Reluctantly, he let her go. Immediately, he missed her closeness and wanted to take her back into his arms, to smooth the strain off her pretty face. He resisted the impulse, knowing it wasn't the time. Nor did he have the right. Instead, he had to content himself with letting his eyes roam her face, just to assure himself that she was well.

"I'm okay. Really," she insisted as his right eyebrow nudged upward. "Just tired. And aggravated. Was it a bear?"

He wished he could tell her it had been.

Her shoulders drooped as he shook his head. "I don't think so. A hole has been cut in the hedges out yonder." He waved in the direction of the left corner of her lot. She and Tony had planted bushes all around the perimeter of the backyard. Thick bushes that would have been hard to fit through. "A hole big enough for a man to fit through. The branches were lying there, and they had clearly been cut with shears. Someone was here, but Izzy kept them at bay."

Tears welled up in her eyes. Oh, man. He hated to see her beautiful blue eyes filled with tears. It ripped his heart to pieces seeing her in pain. Irene rubbed the tears away, then knelt and gave the blond Labrador a hug. Izzy returned the favor in the form of doggy kiss with her wet tongue.

"Oh, yuck. Thanks, Izzy." Irene leaned her head back to consider Paul. "Don't take this the wrong way. I'm glad you showed up. But why are you here? Where is the officer on duty?"

He grinned.

"I *am* the officer on duty. We are short-staffed, remember? I have two new hires that will be starting next week. Until then, we're making do. I have my shaving kit and a change of clothes for church in the car."

She grimaced.

He hesitated. "Or we could stay here if you'd feel safer keeping indoors?"

She vehemently shook her head. "No. I feel like I need to get out of here for a few hours. And it's church. What could happen there?"

FIVE

The church had changed since she'd last been inside it. Minor things. It had been painted, undergone some redecorating, and the social hall had been remodeled. It was easier to focus on these details than on what was happening around her.

Her emotions were a roller coaster. When Paul leaned over to grab the hymnal, she found herself inhaling deeper, enjoying the scent of his understated cologne. Realizing what she was doing, she jerked away from him. He gave her a quizzical look. She busied herself looking around, trying to ignore the heat rising up her neck and cheeks.

After the service, she found herself surrounded by people welcoming her back into the fold. Although there were those who just wanted to satisfy their curiosity or get some fodder for gossip, most of them were genuinely glad to see her back after so long. She didn't see Melanie and Jace. They had probably gone to an earlier service so he could attend church before he and Miles flew out.

When Paul made a general excuse that they should be on their way because his mother needed to get home, she agreed with alacrity. Disappointed to see her go, but unwilling to argue with the police chief, most of the crowd shuffled back into the aisle to make their way to the doors that led to the outside of the stone church building.

"Thanks for the rescue," Irene murmured as Paul put a warm hand on her elbow and motioned for her and the boys to walk ahead of him. "I never know what to say in situations like that."

"It's okay. I don't know what makes people do that."

Someone jostled her from behind. Irene startled and turned her head to see a strange young man. He gave her an apologetic smile.

It was a bit crowded. It must have just been an accident. She nodded and smiled back. She didn't recognize him, but then she hadn't been here for so long, there were bound to be new faces. She turned back to Paul. He had his phone out.

"In church?"

Okay, so now she sounded like her mother. She was way too young for that.

Paul grimaced, but slid his phone back into his pocket.

"Sorry, just checking on Sergeant Zee. Mary seems to be doing all right. Probably because Zee is a woman. And the red hair might have something to do with it." She hadn't considered it, but if Mary's mother had red hair, it might have been comforting for her—drawing her first to trust Irene, and then to trust Sergeant Zee.

"Any luck finding her family yet?"

"No. I will drive to Spartansburg soon. Take a look around. Want to come?"

Surprised that he would ask, she hesitated.

His face went blank. "You don't have to. I just thought that it would be easier if we could take Mary along, since the Amish community wouldn't be comfortable with us showing a picture of the child. And Zee has something else she needs to attend to."

Regret rose up. She hadn't meant to make him feel bad, but she sensed her hesitation had done just that. "Of course, I want to come. It can't be today, though. My neighbor across the street has her sister visiting today. I promised I would go over for a bit and show them how to set up Skype accounts. The sister is moving out of state."

Paul nodded, looking thoughtful. "What time?"

She shrugged, catching the end of her braid in one hand and twisting it.

"I don't know. Sometime after lunch. She'll text me."

He opened his mouth to say something, then shut it as they neared the pastor. They greeted the man, then scurried to catch up with Mrs. Kennedy and the boys, who were halfway across the parking lot.

Paul opened her door for her, and Irene started to slide into the back seat next to her sons. She looked up and stopped.

"Paul, do you know that young man?"

Paul looked over where she was pointing. The man who had bumped into her in church had been staring after them while talking on his phone. The intensity of his gaze made her shiver. He was now busy talking to some of the older women as they left. The women were laughing. So maybe they knew him. She felt like an idiot.

"I've never seen him before." Paul frowned. He discreetly held up his phone and took a picture of the man. "He could just be someone new to the area."

Irene ducked into the back seat with AJ and Matthew. Paul cast one last look at the man. Then he got in and yanked his seat belt in place.

"Y'all ready?"

They dropped off Mrs. Kennedy first. Irene had expected Paul to take her and the boys home first. Then she remembered. Understaffed. There was no one to keep an eye on them but him. Yeah, she had forgotten about that one. Sighing, Irene sank back against the seat, rubbing her hands against her thighs as she gazed out the window.

"Why don't you move up front?"

It would have been ridiculous to refuse. And she didn't mind sitting next to Paul. Frowning, she changed seats, not sure why she was suddenly feeling so low. She hated to think it was because Paul was spending time with her solely because it was his duty. Because that would mean that she wanted him to spend time with her by his own choice. And she didn't. Did she? She tried to convince herself she wasn't developing renewed feelings for the handsome man beside her.

"Looks like Nola's sister's arrived," she commented as Paul swung his car into her drive. A blue compact car was sitting in the driveway across the street.

"Have you ever met her sister?"

She opened her mouth to reply, but AJ exploded out of the car, Matthew hot on his tail. "Mommy! I'm hungry. Is Chief Paul eating lunch with us?"

Irene chuckled at her guys. They would give the Energizer Bunny a run for his money, that's for sure. "Okay, okay. I can only answer one question at a time. Chief Paul is welcome to eat with us. As long as he doesn't mind cheeseburgers and French fries."

He grinned. "Yum. I will even help you make 'em."

She nodded, shooing the boys ahead of her. "You two change out of your church clothes, then you can have a few minutes of free time before lunch. But stay in the house." Her heart twinged at the way their shoulders drooped, but she needed to keep them safe. That had to be her priority.

"Aw, Mom!"

"Hey, Junior…don't sass your mama." Paul tussled AJ's hair, a crooked smile flashing across his face.

At the familiar pet name—the one her husband had used for AJ—Irene's stomach dropped. She realized she had been enjoying Paul's company and hadn't even thought of Tony until now.

Better get things back on track. "And no,"

she responded to Paul. He looked puzzled. "I have never met her sister. But she talks about her all the time."

The hungry group made their way inside. Soon, the aroma of sizzling meat and baking fries was pungent in the air. Paul set the table while Irene fixed the food. When it was ready, the children were called and they sat down to eat.

It felt like a normal family thing to do, Irene thought with a pang. And Paul was seated at the head of the table as if he belonged there. Tears stung her eyes. She blinked them away. Never had she been so grateful to hear her cell phone ping. *Great timing, Nola.*

"It's Nola. As soon as lunch is done, I'm going to go over."

Paul frowned. He didn't say anything, though, until they were finished eating and the boys were cleaning up the dishes.

"I should go with you," he said in a low voice.

She snorted. Loudly. "Please. Paul, this is my neighbor. And these are plans we made before I was in danger. You can watch me cross the street. And I will text you before I start back. But I don't want to leave the kiddos alone, and they'd just be bored if they came with me."

She could see that he wanted to argue. She lifted her chin and crossed her arms, daring him. After all, she was an adult. And it was daylight. Not to mention the fact that there was a police car in front of her house. Anybody would have to be crazy to try to attack her with the chief of police just across the street.

She knew she'd won when he sighed.

"Fine. Do me a favor, though. Give me a thumbs-up when you get there to let me know everything's good."

Irene rolled her eyes. It sounded like something she would tell her boys when she dropped them off at a friend's house. Not like something you'd tell a woman who was almost thirty. Still it was sweet, in a way.

Grabbing her phone, she put on her coat and headed across the street.

Humming under her breath, she rang the doorbell. And waited. When no one answered, she shrugged and frowned. The doorbell must not be working. She knocked. Footsteps crossed the wooden floor just behind the door. Finally. She'd been starting to worry. The door opened.

"Hi—" The greeting that was ready on her lips died as she spotted the person standing behind sweet little Nola.

The young man Jace had identified in the

police station. The one who had been watching her.

"You took long enough. Get in the house. Now."

The impulse to scream or throw some sort of fit was strong. Anything to let Paul know something was wrong, that she had walked into a trap. But she couldn't. Because he was holding a gun.

And it was pointed right at Nola.

Paul had watched from the doorway, growing increasingly uneasy the longer the door stayed unopened. The women were expecting Irene. What was the holdup, anyhow?

But finally the door opened, and Paul had seen the older woman standing in it. She looked frail from his position.

Why wasn't Irene going inside? She was a target out here.

And why wasn't she giving him a thumbs-up?

After an eternity, she began to move inside the house. He sighed in relief, glad she was getting out of the open. Her hand moved up behind her back to give him the requested thumbs-up.

Only she didn't.

She gave him a thumbs-down.

Then she was inside the house.

What? Something was terribly wrong. Paul grabbed his cell phone and called for backup. He started for the door, ready to dart across the road. Wait. The kids were in the house.

What could he do? He couldn't wait to go after Irene. She'd obviously walked into some kind of ambush.

"AJ! Matthew!" The boys came running. "Listen to me. This is very important. Are you listening?"

Both boys nodded, their young eyes flaring wide and anxious at the tone in his voice.

"Your mama needs my help. Now. I have to go across the street. I need you to stay in the house. Lock the doors. Keep Izzy with you and do not open the door unless it's me, your mama or one of the officers that you know. Don't even open to an officer you don't know. Clear?"

"Yes, sir," AJ said. Matthew nodded, his eyes fearful.

Man, he didn't want to scare the kids, but he had no choice. As soon as the door was locked behind him, he was off, running across the street to the house Irene had disappeared into five minutes earlier. He moved around the house, peering in windows. He couldn't risk barging in and maybe getting Irene killed.

The back door was open a smidgen.

He nudged it open a little farther. Weapon out and ready, he slid along the wall. Voices were coming from deeper in the house. An older woman's quavering voice. A man's angry growl. Irene's calming voice—the tone she used to restore peace when her kids were fighting.

A slap. A woman cried out. Irene. The sound of something hitting the floor. Hard.

That was it. Moving quickly, he came to the doorway and peered in. An elderly woman was on the couch, her arms tied behind her at an uncomfortable angle. A young man was standing in the middle of the room. But not just any young man. This particular man's photo was hanging up in the station and had been sent around to other stations in the area. He was standing over Irene, who was in a heap on the floor. And that man was pointing a gun at her, ready to shoot. Rage like Paul had never known surged through his veins. Instead of clouding his mind, though, he saw everything with startling clarity.

"Police! Drop your weapon!" Paul stepped into view, his service weapon held in front of him, trained on the would-be assassin.

With a roar, the man wheeled on Paul and whipped his own gun up. His intent was clear. He had his finger on the trigger. He shot. Paul dodged and the picture behind him shattered.

With a yell, the man pivoted slightly and took aim a second time. This time at Irene.

Paul fired.

The man fell.

Paul knew immediately he was dead. Sorrow struck him. He hated taking a life. Any life. But he knew he'd had no choice. The man had been intent on killing Irene.

Paul replaced his weapon and hurried over to check on the two women. The older woman seemed unharmed though clearly frightened out of her mind. And who could blame her?

Irene was sporting a bloody lip from where she'd been struck. Otherwise, she seemed fine. He crouched down to her level. With a sob, she threw her arms around his neck, almost strangling him. He buried his face in her hair. He had nearly lost her. Five minutes later…

He couldn't bear to even think along those lines. A shudder ran through him.

"Chief!"

With one last deep breath to steady himself, Paul pulled away from Irene. Searching her drenched eyes, he was relieved to see she was calmer. He moved back more, and her arms fell from his neck. Immediately, he wanted to pull her close again.

Instead, he stood.

"In here, Parker!"

Sergeant Ryan Parker entered, his eyes widening as he took in the scene.

"My kids!" Irene bounded to her feet, her expression wild.

"Easy, Irene. They are okay. I had them lock themselves in with the dog. They know not to answer except to one of us."

"Can I go to them?" The words were meek, the expression was not.

He pitied the person who would dare to stand between Irene and her children. He certainly wouldn't. He had Parker escort her back across the street while he stayed to interview Nola. Halfway through the interview, her sister arrived. He had to wait through the new storm of tears. And then the paramedics arrived to check her out. There were no visible injuries, but since she had a known heart condition, they were taking no chances. He would have to visit her later to get the rest of her report.

"Sir, you might wanna see this."

"What do you have, Parker?" Paul slipped on latex gloves from the box Parker had brought with him.

Parker handed him a picture from the dead man's wallet. Paul had already recognized him as Niko Carter, the man who had been watching Irene's house the previous day. His collarlength blond hair made Paul fairly certain that this was one of the men the Zilchers had described. In the photo, Carter was standing next to another young man. Buzz cut. Belligerent stare. Black hoodie with the hood down. The third man from the house? Probably.

Paul called it in. "We know Carter's name and his record, but we're going to need to dig deeper. I want to know everything about him. Down to his shoe size and his favorite cereal. That includes everyone who's given him a job, partnered with him on a crime or shared a jail cell with him dating back to juvie. And I want to know it yesterday."

"Gotcha, Chief. We'll find everything we can."

"You do that, Parker. I am leaving the scene now to head over to Irene's. I want to interview her as soon as possible." *And I want to make sure she and the kids are okay.* He couldn't say that out loud, though. All he knew was that it took every bit of his considerable discipline to carry on as if this were a normal case, when his gut told him to go to her and stay there until the danger had passed. Not happening. Even if she was his best friend's sister, he still had a job to do.

Is that all she is to you?

He shoved the question from his mind. Whatever he had once felt for her was irrelevant. She was in trouble, and he was the chief of police. That was it. It had to be.

Jogging across the street to Irene's house, he kept his eyes roving the street for any signs of other possible dangers. There was no doubt now that she had become a target. The fact that one of the men after her was dead in no way mitigated the danger. There was still one, maybe even two men who were after her.

Some of the tension drained from him when he found Irene sitting with her boys on the couch. Although he could see the fear lurking in the blue depths of her eyes, she was doing a fair job of presenting a calm front to her sons. Still, the two kids were too smart not to have picked up on something. Instead of running around like usual, they were snuggled against each of her shoulders. He knew from talking with some of the officers who had kids that children seemed to have an instinct about what their parents were feeling. According to one of his lieutenants, Dan Willis, it was next to impossible to hide anything from his twin toddlers.

He had long ago accepted that he would remain single, but now, looking at those kids, his felt a pang in his gut at the knowledge of what he would never experience for himself.

Just then, Irene lifted her head. Her gaze

latched on to his. The pit of his stomach dipped, like when he was riding a very steep roller coaster. It was not a feeling he enjoyed at the moment, so he ignored it. He needed to talk with her. Alone.

"Kids, go play in your room while I talk with Chief Paul."

Grumbling, the boys obeyed, their steps sluggish.

As soon as they were gone, Paul perched on the coffee table in front of Irene. He hated the weary look in her eyes. He needed to solve this case so she could relax.

"Irene, are you sure you're okay?"

She nodded. "Just spooked. I don't know how I'll ever step into that house again."

"Don't worry about that yet. Right now, I need to know what happened."

She took a deep breath. "I thought you were being paranoid when you insisted on the thumbs-up. Now I am really grateful." He nodded. So was he. "That guy, he planned to kill us both, so he didn't care what he told us. He said that the boss wanted me out of the way. I had interrupted a very important transaction. Mary had a family waiting for her. They've already paid money, so the kidnappers had to deliver her. I was a target because I had seen the leader's face up close."

Paul bit back the anger swirling in his gut. *Keep calm. Don't let yourself get off track.*

"He probably wouldn't have cared that you'd seen him until he realized you had Mary."

Irene sat up straight. One hand shot out and grabbed his arm. She held on so tight he could feel each individual finger digging in. He kept his face blank.

"Paul! He said they were going to get Mary back! His partner was the man from church—he heard us talking about her staying at Sergeant Zee's and texted the update to him and to their leader. It won't take them long to figure out who Zee is."

Paul pulled his cell phone out of his pocket and punched in Zee's number. "Come on, come on. Answer the phone."

Two rings. Three. When the phone rang four times and went to voice mail, Paul knew something was wrong. He barked out a message, warning her.

He only prayed they weren't too late.

SIX

He needed to get to Zee's place, pronto. But he also knew that he needed to make sure Irene, AJ and Matthew were protected. There were two madmen still out to get her.

Shifting into command mode without thought, he started barking orders to Gavin Jackson the moment he came in the door. It wasn't Paul's normal style of command. He prided himself on his ability to keep his cool even when everyone else was losing it. It was a skill he had honed for years, after life had taught him some hard lessons. He had paid the price once for his lack of control. It had almost cost him his friendship with Jace. And it had cost him any chance he may have had with Irene.

Clenching his fists, he closed his eyes briefly, willing himself to control the anxiety spinning inside him. Then he murmured a quick prayer for guidance and strength. Right now, he desperately needed both.

Opening his eyes, he regarded Jackson, who had come to stand in front of him.

"Sir, a unit is on its way to Sergeant Zee's place. I also have an ambulance on standby."

"Very good, Jackson." He rolled his shoulders and took a deep breath. But then his pager suddenly started beeping. The dispatcher's voice came over the air, announcing an attempted break-in. The intruder was still on the premises. An officer was on the scene, requesting backup. There was a child present, although the dispatcher did not disclose the child's age or gender. She rattled off an address. Paul and Jackson looked at each other.

Dismay was dawning over Jackson's face. It was probably mirrored on his own. He made a decision.

"I'm going to head out that way, see if I can lend a hand. The other unit should beat me there, but I don't want to risk it."

"What's wrong?"

As one they turned. Irene was staring at them, concern furrowing her forehead.

Paul sighed and rubbed the back of his neck. There were so many things to factor in here.

"That call that just came through, that's Sergeant Zee's address," Paul replied. "There's a unit on the way, but I am going to head over there, too. We have no way of knowing how many intruders showed up to get Mary."

Irene lifted her coat from the back of the sofa and shrugged into it. "I'm going with you." Both men started to protest, but she cut them off. "Who else will be able to deal with Mary while you take care of the attackers?"

"We don't have time to argue." Paul faced Jackson. "Who's on duty here to protect Irene and the boys?"

"I guess that would be Parker."

Paul gave a single nod. Parker hadn't been with them that long, but he had already been tested and tried. Paul knew that he could handle watching over the kids. Just to be on the safe side, though...

He picked up his phone and dialed The second ring was interrupted as the call was answered.

"Parker." His voice was confident. Good. Paul needed someone who knew what they were about.

"Kennedy here. I need you to take the boys to their grandmother's house and stay with them there. Jackson will supply the details."

"Understood, Chief. Mrs. Russell just left in an ambulance with her sister, and the ME has removed the body. I'm coming over so Jackson can brief me."

He loved the way his officers worked together.

Paul strode at a brisk pace out to his car, aware of Irene following him. They passed Parker as he was on his way in. A tall man with short light brown hair and dark eyes, Parker looked like a laid-back young man with a carefree grin and a casual saunter. Until you saw him in duty mode. He wore his duty like some men wore aftershave. Effortlessly. Paul saw Irene dissect him with a glance, then smile. Parker had passed the mother exam.

Paul slid into his seat, shaking his head as Irene snapped her seat belt into place. It was, of course, completely insane to have her along on a police call. On the other hand, she had made a very valid point. Mary had been terrified of him previously. He hated to think it was due to abuse she had suffered, but knew it was the most likely scenario. It was essential that they protect the child, but if there was a situation brewing, Irene was the only one he knew of besides Zee who the little girl would allow nearby. If he could avoid traumatizing the child, he would. And that meant having Irene accompany him.

Sergeant Zerosky lived on the edge of town.

While she didn't have neighbors as near as Irene did, there were other houses in the area. The ambulance had already arrived and had pulled into the driveway. Paul fervently prayed for the safety of Sergeant Zee and Mary. There wasn't room to park another vehicle in the narrow drive without blocking the ambulance. He edged his car snug against the curb, directly behind Thompson's cruiser, and put his hand on the door to open it. Before he pulled the handle, he glanced over at Irene. The whirling lights from Thompson's vehicle were splashing across her face.

"I need to know that you will listen to me immediately without asking questions once we're in there. It's the only way I will feel free to go in and do my duty." Irene had never been one to take orders well, but he knew she would do whatever she could to keep a child safe.

"I understand." Her voice was low, intense. He could already see it in her. She was determined to do what he said to protect Mary. Good. They were both on the same page.

Feeling like every second could mean life or death, Paul waited for Irene to exit the vehicle. When he realized that his fingers were tapping an impatient rhythm against his thigh, he forced himself to hold his hand still. As soon as Irene reached his side though, he grabbed hold of her hand and pulled her along toward the house.

He was slightly embarrassed when he reached the house and realized that he was still holding her hand. And even more embarrassed when he realized how perfect her hand felt in his. But now was not the time to be noticing things like that. He had a child to save and an officer at risk.

When he reached the front door, he started to call out, then paused. Voices were coming from the deck at the back of the house. What were they doing outside?

Refusing to allow himself to hesitate, Paul continued at a brisk pace through the house to the sliding door in the rear that led onto the deck. He paused. He could clearly see Sergeant Zee, lying down on the deck but conscious, although she seemed a little out of it. And judging from the fussing baby noises drifting down from upstairs, Mary was present and alert. He could see the blue uniform of a paramedic on the stairwell. The paramedic glanced back at him and gave him a thumbs-up. Okay. So he didn't need to worry about the baby for the few minutes. A second paramedic was kneeling on the ground next to his officer. On the other side of Zee was Sergeant Thompson. When Thompson spotted his chief, he murmured something to the paramedic and headed their way. Paul opened the sliding door to let him in.

"Paul," Irene whispered. "I want to go upstairs and check on the baby. Make sure she's okay."

"No need for you to do that, Mrs. Martello," Thompson assured her in his comforting voice. "The other paramedic is checking on her right now."

Irene compressed her lips together. If Paul were to guess he would say that she was biting her tongue to keep from arguing. Poor Irene. He knew her desperate concern for the little Amish girl was tearing her up. Still, he couldn't let her place herself in danger until he knew the scene was safe. He turned his attention on Thompson.

"Report, Sergeant."

Sergeant Thompson straightened. "It's like this, Chief," the officer began. "The intruder was neither the man that Jace had pointed out nor the bearded man you described."

Realizing that Thompson wasn't up-to-date on the information, he quickly filled him in on Carter's death. When he mentioned the other man that had been in the picture with Carter, Thompson pursed his lips and nodded. "Yeah, that seems about right. The intruder was young, and from what I could tell had dark hair. Medium build, but strong. He ran out the back door and jumped over the fence when I arrived. Sergeant Zee managed to Tase him, but he had already snuck up behind her and struck her pretty hard on the head. The paramedic thinks she probably has a concussion. He didn't have time to get to the child."

Well, that was something to be grateful for. As much as he wished the intruder had been caught, it was good to know that he could focus on one person without putting the other in danger. He turned and caught sight of Irene.

Her arms were crossed and her foot was tapping the floor. She was the very picture of impatience, possibly irritation. Being told that she couldn't go check up on a crying child had to go against the grain. But the baby was in good hands and didn't seem to be hysterical, even though he could still hear her fussing.

"I'm going to go talk with Sergeant Zee," he informed her, ignoring the storm clouds gathering on her brow. "Do me a favor, will you? Stay here until I get back. You can be my go-between if the paramedic needs anything."

He waited for her agreement. It was slow in coming, but he couldn't leave without knowing she'd remain where she was. She nodded, reluctance stamped all over her pretty features. That didn't matter. As long as she was safe, he could deal with whatever annoyance she was feeling.

Irene stood, indecision cluttering her mind. On the one hand, Paul had told her specifically to stay here. And it wasn't like she was needed upstairs at the minute. The paramedic was with Mary. And the little girl was making normal babbling noises. Plus, the attacker had scampered over the fence. So there was no need to be anxious.

But she was. Despite telling herself not to be silly, she couldn't stop the tremors that reverberated deep in her soul and made her stomach queasy. It was like being behind the wheel of a race car zooming out of control and off the track and then discovering that the brakes have failed. She knew she wanted the horror to stop and was powerless to make it happen. And that powerlessness tore at her whenever she heard anything that sounded like it could be a whimper coming from Mary upstairs while she was stuck down here, unable to do anything to help.

Irene didn't like feeling she wasn't in control. She'd been that way for months after Tony had died. And when she had gotten her life to where she felt it was manageable again, she had promised herself that never again would she allow herself to be in a situation where she felt so inadequate. So weak.

Like she was now.

Shaking her head fiercely, she tried to ward off the dismal thoughts. Feeling sorry for herself wouldn't help. She tapped the glass door. It was a heavy glass. It must have been soundproof, too. She was only a few feet away from the group outside on the deck, but she couldn't hear a word they were saying. Paul was talking now. She could see his lips moving. If she inched open the door, she'd be sure to hear his deep voice. She liked the way he talked, in that slow, comforting drawl. What was the word she was searching for? *Smooth.* That was it.

Smooth as hot fudge over vanilla ice cream, a friend had once described it. Irene rolled her eyes at the memory.

Thump.

Irene startled, her eyes shooting to the ceiling. Something had fallen. Something heavy. Mary was up there. No, Mary wouldn't make a crash like that. And she was in her crib.

Remembering how Matthew had managed to climb out of his crib at fifteen months, Irene wasn't reassured.

She didn't need to worry. There was a paramedic up there with her.

A second later, Mary started crying.

That wasn't a cry. That was a more a scream… of terror.

Forgetting her promise to Paul, Irene shot up the stairs without any thought to the possible danger. The sound of her steps was drowned out by Mary's howls. There was a baby upstairs who was hurt, terrified or both.

Irene reached the top of the stairs and pivoted to the right, toward the shrieks. And nearly stumbled over the body of the paramedic.

She very nearly lost her lunch right then and there. She didn't need a medical degree to know the man was dead. There was a hole in the middle of his forehead, and his eyes were staring straight ahead. She hadn't heard a gun, but she knew about silencers. She'd just never seen one—or the effects of one—up close before.

Paul. She needed Paul.

Mary shrieked again. Hysterical.

"Shut your mouth, brat," an angry voice growled. "Or I will do it for you. I ain't got time for this."

No time for Irene to get Paul. Mary could be dead, injured or gone before he arrived. Irene crept to the door of the room, eyes searching for a weapon the whole time. She passed another room with an open door. It was a bedroom, with a vase full of roses on the nightstand. She grabbed the vase. It was long and slender, shaped like a tube. She picked it up. It was heavy. Probably lead crystal. That would work. She didn't have the luxury of searching for the bathroom to empty it, so she dumped the roses and water in a soggy gush onto the carpet. She grimaced and mentally apologized to Zee, but she had no choice.

Whirling out into the hall, she saw a man heading the opposite direction carrying a straining Mary, her little mouth taped shut. Tears were pouring from her devastated eyes.

It was a man she'd probably have nightmares about for the rest of her life. Black Beard.

"Hey!"

Black Beard jerked back as if scalded. His shock didn't last long. He swung in Irene's direction. Recognition flared in his dark eyes. His beard parted in the most hideous grin. It was filled with triumph. Irene realized she'd just given him the other thing he wanted aside from Mary—her.

Dropping the struggling toddler onto the floor beside him, the man surged toward Irene with a roar, huge arms open to grab her. Mary sat up, her little hands moving to the tape on her face. Irene pulled back from the man, but he still managed to grab a handful of her jacket. With a fierce yank, she pulled the slippery material from his meaty hands. He growled. Lunged again.

Acting on instinct, Irene tightened her fist around the vase. With a heave, she swung her arm around, slamming the side of the lead-crystal vase into the side of Black Beard's head with a satisfying clunk. The vase hit the floor. He staggered. Shook his head.

Irene hoped he'd stay distracted long enough for her to grab Mary and escape. She darted around him, putting herself between the toddler and her kidnapper. The child's small arms reached out for Irene. Unfortunately, Black Beard didn't remain stunned for long. Whirling, he fixed his eyes back on Irene.

Rage distorted his features.

Now what? She was literally stuck in the middle with nowhere to run.

"Irene!"

It was Paul! He must be looking for her.

The man whipped his gaze toward the stairs. He reached back and pulled a gun with a silencer on it from his waistband.

"He has a gun!" she shouted in warning. Grabbing Mary, Irene rushed back into the bedroom and slammed the door, locking it. Then she dove to the other side of the room, the weeping child still in her grip, seeking shelter.

And not a moment too soon. The lock of the

door splintered, great chunks of the wood blowing inward. Black Beard had shot out the lock.

"Police! Surrender your weapon!"

Paul. *Oh, Lord. Please keep him safe.*

The prayer came out naturally. Because she knew only God could help.

Several more explosions in the hall. Gunfire. Then more crashes.

It wasn't until Mary patted her face that Irene realized she was weeping. For whom she didn't know. Mary? Paul? The paramedic? Maybe even herself. Or all of them. All she did know was that she was desperate to see if Paul was safe. But she knew she couldn't leave Mary alone. Mary. The sweet baby still had a piece of tape over her mouth, although she had worked it off enough so that she could breathe. Irene pulled it off the rest of the way, trying to be gentle.

Hugging the child close, Irene waited, her mouth dry. She tried to swallow past the lump in her throat. It was torture not knowing what was coming. The sound of running feet pounded past the door. But not toward the stairs, like she would have expected.

Her breathing sounded like a freight train to her own ears in the silence. She'd never really thought of silence as loud before. Now she longed to hear something to tell her that Paul had survived.

"Chief!"

"Up here, Thompson."

The sound of Paul's voice sent a flood of relief through her. Her spine went soft, and she wilted against the wall, bringing Mary with her. The baby laid her unbonneted head against Irene's chest, sticking her thumb into her mouth and gently sucking.

"Irene? Irene!" Paul called, his voice frantic.

"We're fine," she yelled back. "I'll be there in a moment."

She half expected him to charge through the door, but then she heard another pair of feet stomping up the stairs.

"Is that...?"

"Yeah. He's dead. The intruder shot him point-blank, looks like."

They must be talking about the murdered paramedic. Irene felt sorrow for the man, wondering if he left a wife behind, or children. She knew all too well the suffering that they would go through.

"What about Jace's sister? And the kid?"

"She's fine. Said she'd be right out." His voice was calm, but she detected a slight edge to it. He was concerned. She needed to move.

Bracing herself with the wall, she stood.

When she tried to set Mary down briefly, the child wound her chubby arms around her neck, burying her wet face into Irene's shoulder.

"Okay, then. I guess I won't put you down. Come on, Mary. Let's go."

Irene took one step. Paul pushed the busted door open. His skin had an ashen cast to it. At first, she thought he'd been hurt, after all. When he strode forward and pulled her and the child into his arms, she realized he'd been as concerned about her as she had been for him.

Strangely, Mary made no fuss in his embrace. Maybe because Irene was still holding her.

"Are you two really okay?" Paul pulled away, his gaze roaming over them.

"Fine. More scared than anything."

"I had no idea you were in trouble until I came inside and you were gone. Then I heard a crash."

She nodded. "He had shot the paramedic. But he must have used a silencer. And he taped Mary's mouth shut. Did you shoot him?"

She shuddered. She didn't think she could stand seeing one more dead body in the hallway. She was pretty sure she'd collapse into hysterics before the day was through.

Paul shook his head. "No. He ran into the room at the end of the hall and slammed the door. When I got in there, he'd already climbed out the window and down the ladder leaning against the side of the house. I imagine that's how he got in. I think the other guy was supposed to be the lookout while he got Mary."

It made sense.

"I'm taking her home with me."

She waited for the argument. It never came.

"Probably a good idea. And we'll keep a strong detail on your house. Which means that until further notice, you will have someone with you at all times. In the next day or so, we'll take Mary into Spartansburg and start searching for her family."

Relieved that he hadn't tried to dissuade her, she merely nodded.

"Irene…" She looked up, her relief fading at his drawn features. His voice held no trace of its usual drawl. "I don't have to tell you that this isn't over. We know for a fact that there are now two people, at least, after Mary. And they also want you out of the picture. Probably because you are the only real witness. We haven't been able to get a good description of the man who went after Zee. And the second man, the one with the beard? We still haven't identified him. As far as we can tell, he isn't in our database.

We have nothing on him. I suspect he's going to want to keep it that way. And he's willing to kill to make it happen."

SEVEN

The next morning, Irene checked on Mary in the crib that she'd asked Paul to bring down from the attic. It was a school day, so her boys were both up. In fact, the two rascals peeped over the edge of the crib, fascinated. It amused her. It wasn't as if they'd never seen a baby girl before. They hung out with their cousin Ellie all the time. And Lieutenant Willis's wife, Maggie, often brought her twins over to play when the women got together.

Maybe it was because the poor thing was away from her mother. Or maybe it was because Irene was acting like her mother until the little girl's family was found. Either way, they were drawn to her.

"Mommy," AJ whispered, "are her mommy and daddy with my daddy?"

She froze. She hadn't allowed her mind to go there. All at once, emotion swamped her. "I don't know sweetie. I don't think so. But Chief Paul and I are going to find out."

He nodded, not taking his eyes off the sleeping girl.

Irene hustled her boys out of the room, but didn't close the door. She wanted to know if Mary woke up, and she didn't have a baby monitor anymore. The boys got dressed and ate their breakfast. She waved at them as they hurried to get on the bus. Deeper in the house, she could hear Paul's voice. She'd let him in right before checking on Mary. Was he on the phone? In the kitchen, she found Paul talking quietly to Seth Travis—Maggie's half brother. He was a good friend to most of the police department. He was also a paramedic. She heard the words "funeral" and "widow" and cringed. They were talking about the paramedic who'd been killed. Her heart broke for his family.

Before her thoughts grew too maudlin, she caught sight of two shopping bags Seth was holding. He broke off his conversation with Paul when he noticed her and moved her way.

"Hey, Irene. You okay after your ordeal yesterday?"

She smiled. She'd always liked Seth. "Yes, I'm fine, thanks. I'm sorry about your friend."

He compressed his lips, nodding. "Yeah. Me, too."

He hefted the bags in her direction, clearly not wanting to linger on the depressing subject. "Jess and I got these from Rebecca, Miles's fiancée. Her brother collected them for her." Something Amish, then. Rebecca's brother was still firmly entrenched in the Amish community, though he remained close to his sister, who had chosen a different life. And since Rebecca was best friends with Jess, Seth's wife, it made sense that he'd been the one to bring over the package.

"Did she say if anyone had mentioned a missing child?" It would be wonderful if they could find Mary's family right away.

Her hope was dashed as he slowly shook his head. "No. Sorry. But that doesn't mean that a family living on the outskirts of town couldn't have had a child kidnapped. This wasn't a church week, so there are plenty of families her brother said he hasn't had contact with in the past week or so."

Irene recalled hearing that the Amish went to worship services every other Sunday. They didn't have them in a church, but in community members' barns.

Taking the bag that Seth offered her, Irene held it open. Inside were several simple dresses like the ones that the Amish children she'd worked with wore. And a few bonnets.

"Tell her thank you. I think it would mean a great deal to Mary's family."

Seth nodded in acknowledgment and took his leave. "Jess and I have plans with my family this afternoon."

In the wake of his departure, she noticed Paul frowning as his dark eyes scanned over her. "What?"

"Are you sure you're up to this?"

She was slightly insulted. She wasn't a weakling. She'd dealt with hardship before, although never what Mary's family was contending with. It was her duty to help.

"Yes, of course I'm up to it." She couldn't help it that her voice came out a little sharp. It stung that he'd doubt her.

Paul stepped closer. She watched his hand raise, mesmerized as he slid the backs of his fingers down her cheek. "Irene, I didn't mean it to insult you. It's just that you have been attacked three times now in such a short time."

For a moment, she allowed herself to remain still, close enough that she could feel his warm breath on her face, smell the cinnamon gum he'd been chewing. But just a moment. Then she forced herself to step back.

"Right," he said. Was that disappointment? "Let's head out. We have a long day ahead of us."

Irene hurried to rouse Mary, who grumbled but allowed herself to be cleaned up and dressed. One of the dresses fit her perfectly. With care, she braided Mary's hair and put on her bonnet. She was adorable. And hungry. Mary's stomach was growling so Irene fed the tiny girl a simple breakfast and got together both a small ice chest with water and snacks to sustain them throughout the day and a backpack to act as a makeshift diaper bag. Was she forgetting anything? It had been several years since she'd needed to do this, and she was out of practice.

As she moved to the kitchen, the phone rang. She paused, apprehension heavy in her gut. Who would call at seven thirty on a Monday morning? Either something bad had happened, or…

Shaking her head as if she could dislodge the notion, she walked over to the phone and looked at the number display. Not a number she knew. She felt a moment of relief that it wasn't the school or her mother calling to report bad news, but anxiety quickly took its place as the answering machine clicked on and she waited to hear what the caller would say.

Paul stood in the doorway, his face confused. She'd never told him about the calls she'd received the other night. He opened his mouth—

most likely to ask why she wasn't answering her phone. She shook her head.

Her voice ended, and it was followed by a beep. There was a pause, then a man's voice. "You won't get away with what you've done. I will make sure of that."

Click.

"Who was that?" Paul growled.

Irene looked at him. If anyone could help her, it was him. He'd already proved that keeping her safe was his priority. The desire to run into his arms rushed over her and was hard to resist.

Something dropped behind her, and both she and Paul whirled toward the crash. Mary had upended a box of CDs Irene kept on the floor near the player and was picking them up one by one, enthralled. No wonder—they wouldn't have been something she would've had access to in the Amish world.

Irene glanced around her house. It was no longer baby-proofed now that both her boys were in school. A frown settled on her face. That was something she'd need to take care of if Mary would be staying with her for long… but she still hoped that wouldn't be the case, for Mary's family's sake.

She sent up a cautious prayer. *Lord, help us find her family quickly.* Being in danger had sure given her a wake-up call to how much she needed God in her life.

Paul was still waiting for her reply. She told him about the phone calls and wasn't surprised when he hit the roof over the fact that she hadn't mentioned them before.

"How am I supposed to protect you when you keep secrets like that?"

She grimaced. He had a point. "I didn't intend to keep any secrets. I truly did forget about the calls when someone started creeping around my house."

Grumbling, Paul walked into the other room. She could hear him talking on his cell phone. When he returned, his usual calm demeanor was back in place. Funny, how she seemed to be the one who kept making him lose his cool.

"Okay, here's what we'll do. I am having your phone calls monitored. If we can trace the caller, that would be great. I would also appreciate if you kept me apprised of any other suspicious attempts to contact you—including through social media or email. Deal?"

"Absolutely." She wasn't a fool.

"Okay. There's nothing more we can do right now, so let's get on the road."

Paul had made coffee and placed it in travel mugs. Irene added cream and sugar to hers, then donned her coat and stuck her gloves into her pockets. Carrying Mary in her arms, with the diaper bag slung over her shoulder, she followed Paul out to his cruiser. She saw him grab the cooler of food she'd packed. When they got to the cruiser, she noticed for the first time that he had a car seat in the back seat. She raised her eyebrow. He shrugged.

"When Seth texted that he'd be coming over with the clothes, I asked him to stop at the hospital and pick it up. They keep them for emergencies. I installed it while you were busy." He opened her door, and she slipped into the passenger seat. A jolt of electricity shot up her arm when her bare hand came into contact with his. Averting her eyes, she scolded herself silently for letting him get to her.

Did he feel it, too? No, she didn't want to know. Still, the temptation to sneak a peek at his handsome profile when he joined her in the confines of the vehicle got the better of her. His face was bland. Which meant he was probably unaffected by her presence.

She was *not* disappointed by that. Definitely not. The last person she wanted to be interested in her was Paul Kennedy.

The route through Spartansburg, Pennsylvania, was one winding curve after another. The main road was paved, but the majority of the smaller roads shooting off from them were dirt and gravel. Many of the signs with the street names were faded beyond readability. Some of the signs were missing completely.

On the way into town, they stopped at several of the farms, getting out and carrying Mary up to the houses to see if anyone recognized her.

"I don't know of any *kinder* that have gone missing," one woman said kindly, her hand resting on the shoulder of her own child, a boy of only five or six. He leaned against his mother's side, wide blue eyes staring up at the strangers.

"Thanks for your time," Paul said, trying to keep the frustration from showing in his voice.

At the next house, Mary put up a fuss when they got her out of her seat, wailing and twisting until Irene set her on the ground to let her walk. Even then, she folded her little arms across her chest and refused to move, a definite pout forming, pushing out her lower lip.

Paul was amazed at how calm and gentle Irene remained, no matter how stubborn the little girl got.

This time, when the small group managed to make it up to the house, the husband and wife were both there. Paul was disappointed but unsurprised when they denied knowing the child.

"You might find someone who knows more

at the diner in town, ain't so?" The young husband glanced to his wife for confirmation.

"Ja." She nodded her head emphatically. "That is a *gut* idea. Many people go through there every day, and some of them are traveling. They might have heard something from another town."

Finally, an idea he could run with. For the first time that morning he felt a bit of anticipation. He thanked the couple, then he and Irene returned a fractious Mary to her car seat. He aimed the cruiser back toward town. Mary continued fussing.

"It's okay, baby," Irene crooned. "I have something for you." Opening the cooler she'd laid at her feet, she dug around inside until she retrieved a green sippy cup with a triumphant "Aha!"

Mary tugged the offered cup out of the Irene's hand and started drinking, making loud slurping sounds.

He snickered, then shot a glance at Irene and was rewarded by a smile that shot his pulse into orbit. When was the last time he'd shared such a simple moment with her?

Reality crashed down on him. He knew he had feelings for her, but he couldn't allow them to grow. There was too much baggage in his past for a classy woman like her. Plus, once she knew of his secret battles, she might be repulsed. And he wouldn't blame her. Not one bit. He returned his eyes to the road ahead.

Ten minutes later, he parked in front of the diner. Irene got out and released Mary from her seat. She put the wiggly child down to let her walk, but kept a tight grip on her little hand. Paul held the door for Irene, then followed her inside.

Letting his eyes adjust for a moment, Paul turned his attention to their quest and began talking with the nearest stranger. Soon, his hope and patience were rewarded. Although no one recognized Mary, a new bit of information came to light.

"I don't know of anyone around here who is missing a daughter with Down syndrome," one woman said, wiping her hands on her simple apron as she left the kitchen area.

"Well, now, hold on, Ruth." A tall, lanky man unfolded himself from the chair where he'd been sitting, enjoying a large breakfast of biscuits and sausage gravy. "I didn't think anything of it before, but remember what Carl said?" He glanced around the restaurant at the mix of Englisch and Amish folk gathered. A couple of the Amish people nodded their heads, troubled frowns gathering on their brows.

A tingle went up his spine. Something had

happened. Something that might just have a bearing on his case and, hopefully, lead them to getting that sweet baby back to her family. Irene was leaning forward, her eyes intent. She was holding Mary again. The child had her head against Irene's shoulder with a thumb in her mouth, sucking loudly. Her other little hand played with a ribbon hanging down from her starched white bonnet.

"What did you hear? Please, anything could help us." He swallowed back his frustration. The hesitation to share information in front of him was obvious. He understood that the Amish felt uncomfortable discussing community problems with the secular authorities, but come on. Surely, everyone would want to work together to get a child home?

"I do not know all the details," one of the Amish men began, drawing his words out slowly, as if weighing each one. "There was an accident at an Amish farm. A fire, I seem to recall. One of the *kinder* couldn't be located after it was out. The whole community searched. It was thought the young one had died in the fire. I recall hearing she had Down syndrome."

Irene gasped, her hands moving to cradle Mary closer. Paul could almost hear her thoughts. She was putting herself in the mother's place. Feeling the grief in her heart. That was one of the things he'd always found so amazing about Irene. She was the most empathetic person he'd ever known. That's why he'd run so fast from her all those years ago. He couldn't risk dragging her down with him.

Now was not the time to reminisce, he scolded himself. Now was the time for action. He needed to get this child home and find the kidnappers before they could hurt either Irene or Mary again.

"Okay, so where can we find this family?" Paul asked, thinking the sooner the better.

The woman named Ruth spoke up. "I don't think they live around here. Samuel?" She looked back at the man who'd talked about the fire.

"*Nee*. Carl Zook had heard about them from his brother. He said they were from Ohio, but he didn't know the family himself."

Ohio. They needed to get back in the car. Even as he thought that, Paul noticed the way Irene's shoulders sank. She would be away from her boys longer. It couldn't be helped. They would do what they needed to.

"Maybe we could talk with this Carl fellow before driving to Ohio?" Irene asked, her voice soft. Mary had fallen asleep.

"*Ja*, that would be a *gut* idea." Ruth nodded. "He keeps to himself. I don't know if he will talk with you. His place is a little out-of-the-way. But Samuel can give you directions."

Samuel grunted, then accepted the paper and pen she handed him. He proceeded to draw a map on the paper. The directions were rather convoluted. Paul would have much preferred to use the GPS, but no one in the restaurant knew Carl's exact address.

This would have to do.

Thus equipped, they thanked the crowd gathered and turned to depart.

"Young man."

Paul pivoted to face Ruth again. He was a bit tickled to be referred to as "young man." He'd started to feel every one of his thirty-two years lately.

Ruth moved to him, her hand gently touching the sleeping child. "Have faith. Gott is *gut*. He will help you. You must trust Him."

Paul was moved. "I do, ma'am. Every day, I do."

She gave a satisfied nod, then shifted her head to assess Irene. "And you?"

Irene bit her lip. Paul really felt for her. He knew from Jace that her faith had taken a beating since Tony had died. He couldn't blame her. His own heart had felt bruised when he'd lost his friend. But he had never lost faith. She had. Would she ever get it back?

"I haven't trusted God for a while," she admitted. Paul was shocked. Irene had always been a private person, especially when it came to her faith. "I thought He had abandoned me. But I am reevaluating that now."

What? Paul felt his jaw drop at this admission. A tiny spark of joy ignited in his heart. He'd been praying for her to find her lost faith for the past three years, but never had he imagined a conversation such as this one.

"*Gut*, child. Gott will not abandon you. You must always remember that. He is always there. Even when we cannot feel Him."

"Thank you." Irene's whisper was rich with feeling.

Paul guided them back out to the cruiser. He almost bumped into a fellow scurrying along the sidewalk, hands deep in the pockets of a camouflage coat. The man mumbled an apology, but never slowed down.

Some people. Paul shook his head, disgusted at the fellow's rudeness, then dismissed it from his mind. Too many other things to focus on.

Irene immediately set about tucking Mary back into the car seat.

He had the oddest sensation that they were being watched. The hairs on the back of his neck prickled. He glanced around in a full circle. Nothing.

He didn't relax.

"Get in the car," he commanded.

Irene was startled, but complied without question. He got in and started the engine. He drove away, constantly looking in the mirrors and searching the horizon.

"Paul, what is it? You're scaring me." Irene followed his gaze, her own face growing pale.

"I don't know if anything's wrong. All I know is that I have the feeling I am missing something. No clue what, though. Keep your eyes and ears open, will you?"

"Always." Irene sighed and settled back in her seat. "So where are we going?"

Paul handed her the map. "Here, you look at it. I can't while I'm driving. Samuel said that Carl lived up past Buells Corners. Hopefully, he'll be able to tell us where Mary's family is. And that will put us one step closer to finding the people responsible for the kidnapping, and for murdering the paramedic yesterday." *The people who are also after you.* He didn't say the last part. "Read the directions off to me."

She did so.

They weren't as bad as he'd thought at first. Within twenty minutes, they were pulling onto the road that should take them to Carl's house.

They swung into his dirt driveway and Paul cut the engine. Everything was still. He would have expected more activity on a Monday morning. The folks back at the diner said Carl worked from home. Some kind of furniture business out in his barn.

His intuition was going haywire.

"Stay in the car."

Without looking to see if she would do as he ordered, Paul left the cruiser, locking the doors behind him. Then he approached the house, one hand over his service weapon so he could draw it quickly if necessary. His feet made tracks in the day-old snow as he climbed the stairs.

The door was open. Not much, only an inch, but more than a person would leave open on a freezing cold December day. He moved to the door, already dreading what he would find inside the old farmhouse. With all his heart, he hoped he was wrong.

"Mr. Zook? Are you home? Hello?" he didn't expect an answer and he didn't get one.

He put his hand on the door and gave it a gentle push. It swung open, creaking eerily on its hinges. Peering inside, he saw an immaculate house sparsely decorated.

He also saw a body on the floor, a pool of blood spreading out around it.

EIGHT

The back door was wide-open.

Whoever had been here had left in a hurry. Probably when they'd pulled up.

Irene! He abandoned his calm and drew his service weapon. Then he raced back outside and off the porch. He ran straight to the car and hopped in. Irene was staring at him, blue eyes wide and alarmed. He didn't have time to calm her. If Carl's shooter had hung around, then she was a sitting duck in the cruiser. Someone standing outside with a gun could pick her off at any moment. It made him want to rush her indoors.

But he had no idea if the shooter was still inside the house, waiting for her.

"You need to stay down. Carl Zook has been shot. I have no idea if he's alive, but I don't want to leave you here as a target. I'm going to call for backup. Corry is only ten miles away. The Corry police can be here in a relatively short time."

Irene's face had lost all color. But she met his gaze squarely. She shocked him by reaching out and placing one slim hand on his cheek. He swallowed and covered her hand with his. If he lived to be a hundred, he would always treasure that small gesture.

"Paul, be careful."

He smiled. It felt wobbly. "I will. But y'all need to get out of sight so I don't worry."

Without another word, she scrambled into the back seat with Mary, unhooked the little girl and brought her down on the floor with her to play a rousing game of patty-cake. The sight mesmerized him. He'd seen her with her boys. She was a wonderful mother. The thought of her sitting and playing with his child, too, sneaked into his mind.

He shoved the thought away. *Enough.* He wasn't accomplishing anything. There were too many blind spots inside the car. Paul let himself out of the cruiser and crouched beside it. Keeping low, he brought out his phone and called the police. He would have to wait for them to arrive before he went over the scene. While he was anxious to check it out, if he got himself shot he'd leave Irene and Mary in more danger than they were in now.

So he waited. And prayed.

By the time he heard sirens indicating the

police had arrived, his leg was cramped. He stumbled against the cruiser briefly when he stood, but managed to steady himself. He saw Irene watching him from her position on the floor. She was so beautiful. Frightened, pale, angry. It didn't matter. Seeing her and knowing she was well was a balm to his soul.

He would do whatever was necessary to keep her safe. It was more than duty. She was a woman in a million, and he would do right by her—as a friend, since he knew he'd blown his chance of them ever being anything more.

"Chief Kennedy?"

He faced the female officer approaching him. "Yes, Officer."

"Lieutenant Nickols," she introduced herself, pointing to the rectangular pin bearing her name. "Have you checked the scene yet?"

As if he were a rookie? He held in a smile. "No, Lieutenant. I have a woman and child in my vehicle. I couldn't risk their lives."

She was surprised, understandably so. Not many civilians were taken to crime scenes. To her credit, she just nodded and began the search with her partner. Between the two of them, they determined that the house was safe.

They also checked on Carl Zook.

"Hey, Chief!" Lieutenant Nickols yelled

out. "This guy's alive! I got a pulse here. Not a strong one, but it's there."

Thank you, Jesus.

While they were searching, the ambulance arrived.

The crew immediately started to work on the injured man.

Before they could load him on a stretcher and transfer him to the ambulance, a buggy rolled into the driveway.

It was getting really crowded now.

Irene and Mary had moved into the kitchen. That way, Paul had a clear view of them as he assisted the local department. He switched his attention from Irene to the woman hopping down from the buggy and running into the house.

"Whoa!" The male officer, Dudak, stepped in front of her, halting her entrance. "This is a crime scene."

"This is my house!" She shoved past him, then stumbled to a stop as she saw the man on the floor. "Dat! What are you doing to him?"

Paul moved forward. "I'm sorry, miss. I came here to talk to your father and found him. He'd been shot." He held up his hands in a placating gesture when her face paled and she looked like she might faint. "He's alive! Do we have your permission to transport him to the hospital? He will die if we don't."

Boy, he hated to be so harsh.

As he was talking, she went down on her knees next to her father and began to sob. A hand landed on Paul's arm. Irene. She squeezed his biceps. He could feel the warmth of her hand through his shirt. "I'll help," she whispered plopping Mary on the floor with a couple of toys she pulled out of the bag on her shoulder.

As he watched, she went down beside the young woman, putting her arm around her shoulders. She whispered to her. The woman struggled to control herself and listened. Finally, she wiped her tears and nodded.

Irene cast a look back and winked. Paul smiled. Was there another woman who could even compare to her? He doubted it. She amazed him with her strength and her compassion.

"It's okay," she called, obviously unaware of the completely inappropriate thoughts flying around in his head. "She'll let you take him to the hospital."

The ambulance crew didn't waste any time. Within minutes, Carl was loaded into the ambulance and headed to the nearest hospital.

His daughter prepared to follow. As she

stood in the doorway, she paused. "I'm sorry. What did you want to talk to my *dat* about?"

Paul hated to add to her concern. Especially since Carl may have been shot because he had knowledge about Mary. Somehow, someone had clued in to the fact that he and Irene were coming to talk with the man. He was sure of it. Paul didn't have a shred of evidence, but his instincts told him he was dead on target.

"This child." Irene beat him to it. "She was kidnapped and we're trying to find her family. We think her name is Mary. The people in town thought that she may belong to a family in Ohio. A family that thought she'd died in a fire last week."

"*Ja.* I know that story. They lost their youngest daughter, Mary Ann Lapp."

Mary stopped playing on the floor and stood. She walked over to the woman and smiled. Paul caught his breath. He exchanged excited glances with Irene. They were finally getting somewhere.

Paul squatted down beside the toddler. She backed up a little, still a little shy around him and men in general, no doubt. "Mary Ann?"

Her sweet face split into a wide grin, blossoming like a flower in the sunshine. His heart melted. Then she brought her shoulders up and giggled, and he was enchanted.

"It's nice to meet you, Mary Ann."

She giggled again.

He heard a sigh. Irene. When he looked up, there were tears in her eyes. Alarmed, he stood and took her hand. "Irene? You okay?"

"Right as rain." She laughed and wiped her eyes with her free hand. It was amazing how ebullient he felt just because she hadn't pulled away from him. "Silly of me, I know. But it seems like we might actually find her parents."

Without thinking about it, he leaned forward and touched his lips to her forehead. That was really stupid. But it had felt right.

She blinked up at him.

He didn't give her time to decide if he'd gone too far.

"I believe we will find them, Irene. God has a plan for Mary Ann. Just like He has one for you and me." Huh. He probably should have phrased that differently. That sounded like God had a plan for them as a couple. He liked the sound of that more than he should.

Miss Zook was already nodding vigorously.

"*Ja.* Gott has a plan. You have to trust Him."

Irene shook her head, her expression bemused. "I'm trying. In the meantime, do you know where we might find Mary Ann's family?"

"Well, now, I don't know the family myself. Somewhere in Holmes County, I know that much."

Paul could see the discouragement starting to take root inside Irene as Miss Zook hurried out the door, anxious to go with her father. Officer Dudak escorted her to the ambulance.

Mary Ann was occupied for the moment, fascinated by the dust motes dancing in the stream of light coming through the window. Every so often, she'd try to catch the particles, then laughed when she couldn't. What a wonder the world was to a child. He almost envied that simplicity.

He looked up, and was startled to see Irene fighting tears.

"Irene?" She'd been so happy just a second before.

She wiped her eyes. "Sorry. I'm glad that we're getting somewhere, but my heart aches at what her parents are going through."

He took advantage of the child's distraction to comfort the woman.

Gently, he pulled Irene into his arms, ignoring the startled glance he got from Officer Dudak, returning from outside. What did he care for that man's disapproval when someone—a very special someone—was hurting inside?

Irene held herself stiff for a moment, arms

crossed in front of her like a shield. He wasn't giving up. He held her close with one arm across her back. The other hand rubbed slow circles up near her neck. He was rewarded when she relaxed, leaning her head against his shoulder.

For a moment, he forgot his intentions as the sweet, airy aroma of her shampoo assaulted his senses. He had started to lower his head, to breathe in her scent, when realization rushed upon him with a chill. What was he doing? He had no right to feel this way about a woman of her caliber.

But he did.

What was she doing?

Irene felt a change in the way Paul held her. Tension emanated from him. Embarrassed heat flooded her face at the idea that he might think she had read too much into his actions.

She wasn't the vulnerable girl he'd known so many years ago. She was made of stronger stuff and could handle whatever was thrown at her, thank you very much. Hadn't she already proved that?

She pulled out of his arms abruptly. He let her go, his arms dropping to his side. Did he look hurt?

"I'm good," she announced.

His dark gaze roamed her face, questioning. She shivered.

"Irene." Paul's voice was low, keeping his words private between the two of them. "I promise I won't give up. We will keep searching for her family. It might take some time, but we will find them."

She swallowed, transfixed by the intensity of his voice. She believed him. In that moment, it was so clear. No matter what had happened so many years ago, she trusted him now. It would be so easy to fall for him, deeper than when they were teenagers. He had become a man who kept his word and who served those around him tirelessly.

He was also a cop.

That was the thing, the one thing, she couldn't overlook. No matter how her stomach fluttered in his presence or how safe he made her feel, she couldn't—wouldn't—put herself or her children through that torment again.

Ignoring the sorrow bubbling up inside, she took a step back. She needed to put space between them.

"Irene…" Paul shook his head and sighed. She had the feeling he knew exactly what she was doing. "I need to touch base with these guys." He jerked his thumb in the direction of the Corry officers.

She raised her eyebrows.

"They can keep us in the loop on what they find. And I need to be in on the interview with Carl if and when he wakes up. He might be able to give us some details, both on Mary Ann's family and on the man who shot him."

Irene frowned. "Do you think it was the man who was staring at us at church?"

Paul considered. "Yeah, I do. He was in the picture with Carter, and, like I said before, I think he phoned Carter to tell him we were coming. I also believe he was the man who attacked Sergeant Zee."

Irene clenched her jaw in frustration. When would this awful ordeal end? And how many more good people would be hurt before then. She nodded toward the others. "Go ahead."

He touched her hand, then sauntered over to talk with the other officers.

She wanted to scream, she was so frustrated. *Why, God? Haven't I been through enough?* Unbidden, verses came to her mind.

Blessed be the God and Father of our Lord Jesus Christ, the Father of mercies and God of all comfort, who comforts us in all our affliction so that we will be able to comfort those who are in any affliction with the comfort with which we ourselves are comforted by God. For just as the sufferings of Christ are ours in abundance, so also our comfort is abundant through Christ. 2 Corinthians 1:3-5.

Wow. She couldn't believe she remembered that—she had learned it so long ago. But the question was did she believe it? Where was God when she had been trying to put her life back together? Where was He when her babies asked for their daddy? Or when she lay alone in her bed at night weeping for her husband? God hadn't comforted her then.

Because you would not let Him.

The stark truth of that thought hit her hard. She had hardened her heart to God. Whether deliberately or not, she had turned away, refusing to accept His comfort. His strength. Oh, she still would have suffered even if she'd kept her heart open. There was no escaping that. But she recalled vividly the comfort her family had taken in the knowledge that they would see Ellie again after her sister's death. How they had stood together.

She had rejected it all when Tony died. Suddenly, she was ashamed of herself. What kind of example was that for her little ones?

God, I am so sorry for shutting You out. I know danger is stalking me now. Help me to rely on You, no matter what happens.

Peace flowed into her, like a balm on her raw spirit.

A hand tugged at her pant leg…followed by a whimper. Mary Ann.

She squatted down to put her eyes on a level with the little girl. Mary Ann whined again, then patted her mouth. She was so cute in her little white bonnet.

"You're probably getting hungry, aren't you, sweetie?"

The cooler was in the car. Maybe she should go get Paul before running outside for it? He was deep in serious discussion with the officers, though.

Mary Ann whimpered again. What should she do? She'd overheard the other two officers talking a bit ago. They had said they didn't think the perp had hung around. Did that mean the danger had passed? After all, they had checked all the buildings, and had seen no sign of the shooter. Not to mention how long she and Paul had sat in the car without being attacked. Why would the shooter stick around with so many cops roaming through the house and property? She looked down again into Mary Ann's pleading eyes.

She needed to get her food.

"Okay, Mary Ann? I need you to stay here, okay? I'm going to get you some food."

Mary Ann babbled something. Whether it was just baby babble or Pennsylvania Dutch,

Irene had no clue. But she needed to know that the Amish child understood her.

"Can you sit down? Right here?"

Mary Ann plopped down on her bottom, wobbling a bit as she did so.

Relief coursed through Irene. The child understood. "Okay, honey. You stay here. I will be back quickly with something to eat."

She stood and walked to the front door. Paul and the officers had moved to the kitchen. She could hear them talking. The words "forced entrance" and "probably didn't know the perp" floated to where she stood. Poor Carl. To be taken unaware in the supposed security of his own home.

She slipped through the door. If she was quick, Paul would never know she'd gone to the car. She raced across the lawn to his cruiser. Opening the passenger door, she reached in and grabbed the lightweight cooler.

She had just straightened when the first shot came. It slammed into the door she'd been holding on to.

Irene screamed. Dropping the cooler, she darted behind the vehicle, chased by the sound of shot number two. She ducked down low and did a funny squatting walk along the rear of the cruiser, keeping her head below the trunk line. Her hands skimmed the cold bumper to help her keep her balance. Shot number three. The right rear tire took the slug, hissing as the air whooshed out.

"Irene!"

Paul.

He and Dudak raced out. Nickols was probably keeping Mary Ann inside, safe.

"Irene! Where are you?"

Paul called again. She could hear the fear rumbling in his deep voice. He couldn't see her, she realized.

"I'm behind your car!" she yelled back, still keeping low. "I'm fine."

Besides being scared out of her wits, that was.

The Lord is with you, she reminded herself. *Lord, please protect us all. Keep Paul safe.*

For even now, he was racing toward the back of the car, his eyes searching the horizon, service weapon ready. He dashed around the car to the back end. He slipped the arm not holding the gun around her and squeezed.

"You okay?" he queried urgently, gaze skimming over her. His face, she noted, was pale.

Ouch. She hated that she was the one to cause him such fear.

"I'm fine. Terrified, but unhurt."

She waited for the lecture. She even wanted it, because she knew it would be well deserved.

What she got, however, was another squeeze and a kiss on the forehead.

They waited for another shot.

None came. She could hear Mary Ann screaming inside the house. Instinctively, she tried to stand, to go and comfort the child, but Paul wouldn't let her move. Reluctantly, she agreed. Mary Ann was hungry and scared, but she was safe. They were not. Not yet.

After ten minutes with no more shots, Paul called the other officer over. They kept Irene sandwiched between them and, gripping her elbows, fast-walked her back to the house. Their service weapons were out, and they were focused on the trees.

The moment Irene was inside, Mary Ann rushed at her. Irene realized with a pang of regret that the cooler was still outside, on the snowy ground where she'd dropped it. She wasn't about to go after it.

Paul and Dudak turned to the door.

"Wait, Paul! Where are you going?"

He was so busy scanning the trees he didn't even look her way. "We need to search the tree line."

Before she could protest, he was gone. Chasing after a killer.

NINE

Paul motioned Dudak to split off to the left. If this criminal had any brains he'd be long gone by now. Really, he should have left as soon as Paul's cruiser pulled up to the house. Instead, he'd stuck around long enough to go after Irene again. It wasn't smart or logical. In fact, it spoke of someone more concerned with a personal vendetta than keeping under the radar.

Paul zigzagged through the trees, his eyes constantly scanning the brush and the treetops for any sign of movement. Any noise that might lead them to the killer's hiding spot.

Paul already had a pretty good guess what the man looked like. He thought back to the picture in Niko Carter's wallet. That dark-haired guy and the bearded man were after Irene. He had a feeling this was no longer just about Mary Ann.

The search was fruitless.

No sightings. No clues. Nothing that led

them nearer to closing the case and stopping the people who had Irene in their sights.

After about an hour, they had to admit defeat. The shooter had managed to elude them. Again. Paul was starting to get pretty irritated at showing up too late. As he walked back to where Irene was waiting, he kept going over the day's events in his mind.

How had the shooter known that they were going out to talk with Carl Zook? It seemed like too much of a coincidence that he was shot the same day that they would come asking questions—just minutes before their arrival. Somehow, the sniper had made the connection that they would come after him.

Again, the question reverberated in his mind. How?

He had found a way to spy on them and knew that they would be coming out to talk with people about the case today. Had the cruiser been bugged? He'd better search his vehicle, just in case.

Ten minutes later, he frowned in frustration at his car. Nothing. Suddenly, the image of the young man slamming into him outside the diner crossed his mind. It no longer seemed like a coincidence. If he'd gone back inside, it was possible that the locals were still talking of Zook. Yeah. That would fit. He'd left after them, but if the man knew the area well, he might have been able to take a quicker route.

From the yard, he could hear Mary Ann hollering. He spotted the cooler lying upside down on the ground and mentally connected the dots. The kid must be hungry. That was probably why Irene had come outside in the first place. He paused and listened. Yep. She didn't sound hurt or scared. Just mad. Nothing gets a kid mad like an empty belly. He'd watched his sister's kid enough to have learned that the first rule of peace in the house was to keep children well fed. He detoured slightly and picked up the forgotten cooler before resuming his trek to the house.

Immediately, his thoughts returned to analyzing what he knew about the case. It was what he did best…fitting the pieces together. He was so consumed with the clues rattling around in his mind as he walked into Carl's house that he was unprepared when Irene bounded out of the kitchen and threw herself into his arms.

He was unprepared, but not displeased. Dropping the cooler, for a moment he allowed himself the pleasure of holding her. Just a moment. Then he resolutely stepped back. But he couldn't completely distance himself. One look into those blue eyes swimming with tears, and he was lost again.

"Hey, now." He cupped her face in his hands and used the pads of his thumbs to wipe away the moisture. Then he playfully tugged a lock of her dark red hair. "What's this? I'm fine, Red, just dandy."

"Red." She sniffed and let him catch the slightest glimpse of a smile. "You haven't called me that since high school."

It had slipped out without his permission. A slip like that might make one think his feelings, so long buried, were still as strong as they'd once been. But he knew that couldn't be the case. Irene Martello was way out of his league.

"I was so scared when you ran out there, Paul. What if you'd been shot?"

It was a valid concern. He regretted that she'd had to deal with it, but there was no other choice.

"I'm sorry, but you understand we had to see if we could catch this joker?"

She nodded and some of his tension faded. She seemed to be taking everything in stride. Not something he would have expected from her, which meant he'd probably catch it later.

That was fine. As long as she and Mary Ann were safe.

His phone rang. He grabbed it off the clip on his belt without removing his gaze from the beautiful woman before him, now feeding the little girl. He allowed a grin to escape at the way the kid ate, dropping crumbs everywhere. She must have really been hungry.

"Kennedy here."

"Chief Kennedy." The voice was unfamiliar. She identified herself as a nurse from the hospital. "Mr. Zook woke up as they prepped him for surgery and spoke with his daughter. She is now insisting that she has information for you, and refuses to tell it to the staff here. She will only talk to you. Says it's police business."

"Be there soon."

He disconnected and turned to find the three adults in the room watching him. He didn't want to step on any toes here—this shooting was not in his precinct. But the fact that Irene had been shot at... Well, he dared anyone to try to stop him from finding the creep that had thought that was a good idea. This went far beyond whose precinct it was. And if Miss Zook had information that could help him, he wanted to know it right away.

"Okay, folks." He kept his voice at an easy drawl. No need to antagonize anyone. "The hospital called. Miss Zook is asking me to come there. She has some information. I do believe we should move this party to the hospital. See what she has to say."

Officer Dudak scowled. Before he opened his mouth, Paul knew he'd gotten his hackles raised.

"Now, look here, Chief. This is our area. We thank you for your help, but we can handle it."

Paul raised his hands. He was willing to try to placate the man, but this was one time he wasn't budging. "I'm not trying to home in on your investigation. However—" he indicated the child playing on the floor "—this intersects with one of my cases. I have a cop in the hospital and a murdered paramedic." He drilled Dudak with a stare. "And one of my friends has been shot at multiple times. I think this is a good time to work together."

Dudak raised his brows, then shifted his glare between Paul and Irene. His glance mellowed and his face cleared. "Ah, I see. All right. Can't say I like it, but I get it now."

Apparently, it didn't matter how much he tried to deny it. The other man had picked up on Paul's feelings for the beautiful redhead standing so close to him. Had Irene picked up on the insinuation? She looked startled, then a flush swept into her face. She dipped her head, and her hair swung forward. He could no longer see her face. Was she embarrassed because she knew how he felt? Was there any chance she was feeling the same? Or was she upset at any speculation because she wasn't feeling anything for him?

It didn't matter now. Feelings could be sorted out later. Her safety was the priority right now. And that meant he needed to get to the hospital.

"As soon as I change this tire, I'll follow you guys," Paul stated, promptly ending the discussion. They nodded. Officer Dudak stepped forward to assist. In the span of fifteen minutes, both cars were on the road again.

At the hospital, they found a couple of spots in the side lot. Miss Zook was waiting for them in the bustling hospital waiting room. All around her, people played on iPods or sat texting on smart phones.

As they entered, the energy in the room shifted. People sat straighter and averted their eyes. *Nothing charged the tension in a room like the arrival of three police officers in full gear.* Paul bit back a smile. He wondered if any of the people in the room had a reason to fear the arrival of the police, but let his suspicions slide. People just didn't know how to react to them.

Miss Zook immediately made a beeline to them. Or rather, to Paul. "I need to talk with you."

He nodded. "That's why we're here. Let's step out to the lobby, shall we? It might be more private there."

The small group moved into the area between the two sets of sliding doors. Irene and a babbling Mary Ann trailed behind the cops and Miss Zook. The stream of people passing the doors continued and they received quite a few curious stares, but at least it was quiet. They could converse in relative privacy.

Miss Zook watched Irene for a minute.

"It's okay," Paul assured her. "You can talk in front of Irene."

"Ja," she said, her voice soft. "I was thinking about the *kind.*"

"She was stolen from her home." Paul kept his words gentle. But all of the sudden he thought about his own niece, who was just a toddler. Or Dan and Maggie's twins. The idea of living with the death or the disappearance of a child pierced through him. What if Irene had to do that? He knew her sons were her whole world. He had to banish those thoughts if he wanted to keep his mind clear. "We're trying to reunite her with her parents. I think your father knew something about what was happening."

"I think you are right." The girl wrapped her arms around herself and shivered.

Paul's heart twisted. The poor thing. Did she

have anyone other than her father? She couldn't have been more than eighteen. Old enough to be married, but since she still lived with her father, he doubted she was. Although, since Amish didn't wear wedding rings, he couldn't be sure.

"Miss Zook, what did your father say before he went into surgery?"

Dudak shifted his feet restlessly and opened his mouth as if to speak. Paul shot him a warning glance. The young officer snapped his mouth shut, though he didn't look happy. That was just fine. He could be unhappy, as long as he kept his mouth shut.

Finally, Miss Zook seemed to come to the decision to trust him. "He didn't know the man who shot him. Said he was a strange Englischer. Young. With brown hair and a jacket like hunters wear."

Paul felt another piece click into place. The description matched the young man who'd bumped into him outside the diner. He was right about that connection.

Miss Zook kept talking. "The man said Dat was talking too much. And that he was too late. They'd already got another little girl."

They'd kidnapped another child?

Irene reeled from the horrible news. In her

distraction, she squeezed the child she was holding. Mary Ann squirmed and cried in protest.

"Sorry, honey. I didn't mean to do that." Irene kissed the top of the bonnet and set the wriggling child on the ground. Mary Ann immediately moved away and pulled herself up on the bench stationed against the wall.

"Wait." Paul sounded as shocked as she was. "Do you have any idea where this child was stolen from?"

She was already shaking her head. "*Nee.* I asked, but Dat didn't know. The man said that, then shot him. I think he meant to kill him."

"Yeah, good thing our shooter is a lousy shot." The male officer smirked as he elbowed his partner. She, Irene was happy to note, directed a disapproving frown his way.

Paul gave him the fiercest scowl she'd ever seen on his face. Whoa. She was seeing a side to Paul that she'd forgotten about. He always seemed so in control of himself that she'd forgotten he'd had a temper and no tolerance for cruelty or stupidity.

The officer's comment certainly seemed to fall into one of those categories.

"What?" The officer looked affronted. "All I'm saying is that we're dealing with someone who's not used to using a gun. His target was only a few feet away, but he couldn't kill him. And how many times did he shoot at the redhead there? Yet she wasn't even nicked."

Offended at the tactless comments, Irene was tempted to put him in his place. Paul's expression, however, caught her attention. The scowl had melted into thoughtfulness. Tactless or not, something the man said had resonated with Paul.

"You may be right about that, Dudak."

Even knowing he had a point didn't make her like him any more than she currently did.

"Miss Zook, I am going to talk with the Corry police chief. See if we can't get someone to watch your father while he's here."

Her brow furrowed. "While he's here. When he gets released, I don't think Dat will want Englischers guarding him on his own property."

"That's understandable, but here he's still under our guard."

A minute later, the young Amish woman left to go wait on news of her father's condition. The three cops converged to discuss the next step in the investigation.

It suddenly struck Irene as she listened to the conversation just how exhausted she was. She didn't remember being this drained when Matthew was going through colic. And that was almost three months of limited sleep at night while dealing with an energetic toddler all day long.

Letting the police officers and Paul handle the nitty-gritty details, she moved like a sleep-walker to the bench and sat down beside Mary Ann. The little girl abandoned the umbrella stand she'd been examining and climbed up to sit on Irene's lap. She lifted her little hands and patted Irene's cheeks. Her hands were so soft and cool. Affection welled up inside Irene. And longing. Right at that moment, all she wanted was to go home and hug her boys. Hearing that another child was gone broke her heart.

Mary Ann pushed her hands against Irene's cheeks and drew her head down.

Irene looked into her round brown eyes. "Yes, pumpkin? Do you want something?"

The girl tilted her head and pursed her lips. Her little brow wrinkled. Oh, she was the sweetest little thing.

"Mam?"

Irene hadn't thought her heart could break any more, but hearing that first word she'd ever heard from the child broke through the dam. Tears pooled in her eyes. She blinked them back, not wanting to scare the precious child.

"I know you miss your *mam*, sweetie." She sniffed. Her voice sounded thick and fuzzy. She cleared her throat. *God, please help us find her parents.* "We're going to find her. Paul will get you back to your family."

"Yes, I will."

She hadn't heard him approach. The other officers were leaving. The door swooshed behind them. She raised an eyebrow at Paul. His eyes were soft and deep. And the affection and emotion she saw in them reached out and touched a chord deep in her soul. Shoving such ridiculous emotions away, she lifted Mary Ann off her lap and stood.

"Do you need to stay here and wait for Carl to wake up or something like that?" She hoped not.

He shook his head, his gaze never leaving her face. Warmth crept into her cheeks. She needed to stop reacting like a silly schoolgirl every time he looked at her. It was getting seriously annoying.

"The Corry police will take care of that. They promised to keep us in the loop."

She wanted to wilt. Just melt right into a relieved puddle on the floor. But then she reminded herself that the day wasn't over yet. They might be finished at the hospital, but there was still plenty to do.

"What now?" She pulled herself together and straightened her spine. This was not about her.

It was about the little girl holding on to her leg. The child trusted her to get her home. And Irene would do that. *Paul and I will do that*, she amended. Because she would get nowhere without him. *Or without God.*

Even a week ago that thought would have been scoffed at. But now she realized she needed to hold tight to God to keep her sanity.

Paul smiled, a slight half grin that lifted one corner of his mouth. But it still made her feel better. He lifted a hand as if to touch her, then let it drop.

She was not disappointed, she told herself.

"Now we head back to LaMar Pond. I know we need to travel to Ohio. But I refuse to just drive out there without any idea of where we're going. We're going to see if we can find out more about any families named Lapp that recently lost a child. Or had a severe fire on their property. At the same time, I need to put out some feelers for another missing little girl. Come on, let's go home. You can call your mom on the way."

Finally.

They moved out to the car. Paul hit the button to unlock the doors. Irene didn't wait for him to open her door, instead reaching out and pulling the door wide-open.

She stopped.

"Do you hear something?" She leaned her head toward the car, trying to catch the elusive sound.

It sounded familiar. Like a clock ticking.

Her world stopped as fear held her tight in its grip.

"Irene, move!"

Paul grabbed her hand and yanked her and Mary Ann away from the car. "Run!"

She didn't need to be told twice. They were halfway across the lot when the door blew off the car. Paul grabbed Mary Ann from her and shoved Irene forward. She fell, catching herself on her hands. They were scraped raw on the icy parking lot. She barely felt the pain. Mary Ann was screaming. Paul had wrapped himself around the panicked child as he'd gone to the ground.

Mary Ann was terrified and angry. But she was alive.

Irene looked back and promptly gagged.

The car was still there, smoking. The passenger seat, the seat she'd been about to sit in, was gone.

TEN

There'd been a bomb planted in her seat. Paul was still shaking, fifteen minutes later. He berated himself for not seeing the trap. The car had been out of his line of sight for more than long enough to be tampered with. Knowing that, he should have approached more cautiously. *That's what being consumed with concern for a woman will get you*, he scolded himself.

They were alive, though. He was amazed they were all uninjured. Shaken, but not hurt. He gave praise where it was due.

"Thank You, Jesus, for protecting us."

Irene nodded. "I'm thinking He is watching over us."

Well, at least there was one positive thing about this.

Mary Ann's shrieking had subsided into pitiful crying interspersed with hiccups. She was sitting in Irene's lap, thumb in her mouth. Her bonnet was slightly askew. He reached down and plucked gently at the top, straightening it. Irene smiled and hugged the girl closer.

Security from the hospital poured out of the building. Great. Now they would be stuck here even longer, letting the perp put more and more distance between them. Who knew how completely he'd be able to disappear if they didn't go after him now?

Still, Paul tamped down his impatience as they were prodded and poked by the hospital staff to be sure they weren't suffering any hidden injuries.

By the time they were declared injury-free, the Erie Bomb Squad had arrived. Paul was glad to see Trevor Stone leading the crew. Trevor was a shy young man, but Paul had learned to trust his judgment.

"What do we have, Trevor?" he said as he approached the young man. Trevor raised a hand in greeting and pushed his glasses back on his nose.

"Chief. This is a very sophisticated device. See those wires?" He pointed to the wires hanging out of the car where the door had been. Paul couldn't help it. His glance slid farther to where the passenger seat ought to be. He shuddered. Ten seconds more and Irene would have been there.

Don't go there, man. She's fine. You're all fine. Focus on Trevor. "Okay, yeah. I see them."

Trevor continued. "Whoever this dude is, he knows his explosives—and how to use them with precision. This was designed to take out just the passenger seat. Not the entire car. And it was remotely controlled."

Paul straightened, a new horror blossoming in his chest. "You mean he was here, watching?"

"Yeah, afraid so. He had to have been. The countdown didn't start until he pushed the button."

Paul swiveled his head to check on Irene. She was still there. He nodded at the security guard closest to him, and the man jogged over. "That woman is in danger. You stay right with her."

There may have been something in his voice, but the man didn't argue, just ambled away to stand guard over Irene.

And over his heart.

He did not just think that.

"He waited until Irene was getting ready to sit, and then he pushed the button." It was hard to say the words, but he didn't back down from the challenge. Right now, he was Irene's best chance to survive, and she was counting on him to keep his head in the game.

"That's my guess."

Dudak and his partner stepped closer. At some level he'd been aware of them searching the parking lot. "What can we do, Chief?"

"Search the perimeter. Trevor here will give you the range of the remote. Extend your search past that. Any clues will be helpful."

They jogged out. He turned to the hospital personnel. "Are there security cameras in this section of the parking lot?"

When they admitted that there were, he said he wanted a look at the files as soon as possible.

"Chief."

He turned back to Trevor. The troubled expression on the man's face did nothing to quell the dread brewing inside him.

"Spit it out, Trevor. I need to know what I'm dealing with."

Trevor pulled a section of the explosive device from the car. It looked so harmless just sitting in his hand. Not like something that had the ability to rip a body to pieces.

"This device here? I saw it frequently when I was an EOD specialist for the army."

Explosives ordnance disposal specialist. Paul whistled. That type of job took guts and a rock-steady spirit. Those soldiers saw far too much carnage. Paul's respect for Trevor skyrocketed.

Then he frowned. "You're saying that we are

looking for someone with a background in explosives, possibly ex-military?"

"I'd almost guarantee it, sir."

Great.

He called Parker and had him come to pick up Irene and Mary Ann. Irene started to argue. He placed a finger against her lips, stopping her midword.

"Red, you're tired, and who knows how exhausted that baby is. You both need a good meal and some sleep. And at your house, she can be free to walk around a bit more. I will be there tonight to keep watch. Parker will stay with you the entire time until I arrive, so you'll not be alone."

She nodded, although judging by the expression on her face, she wasn't happy about it. Still, some of the tension had eased from her shoulders when he'd said he'd be at her house later.

Warning signs went off in his brain. The last thing he wanted was for her to grow too attached to him. Too dependent. He didn't deserve that kind of trust. As soon as this case was done, life needed to go back to the way it had been.

Maybe it was about time he let her into the darker side of his past. He cringed, imagining the look of disgust that was sure to grow on her lovely face once she knew the real Paul Kennedy. It wasn't a story he enjoyed telling. The only person alive who knew all of it was Jace. He didn't even think his own mom and sister had figured out the whole truth.

Yet, as unappealing as it was, he needed to tell her.

But not now.

He was relieved when Parker arrived thirty-five minutes later to take Irene home. Thompson arrived, too. Presumably to give Paul a ride back to LaMar Pond when he finished at the hospital. As he walked back to the hospital to view the file from the camera, he saw the tow truck arrive to take his vehicle away.

He stopped and watched it. It was just a car. But right now, it was a reminder to him of just how very precious life was.

This was getting him nowhere. He needed to see if the security cameras had caught anything useful. Only then would he be able to get back to Irene. He could really go for a cup of hot, strong black coffee. The stuff in the thermos he'd made that morning was cold by now. Not to mention he had no idea if the perp had tampered with it. He grimaced. He could really use some coffee. If for no other reason than the caffeine might give him a boost to help him through the next few hours.

When they entered the hospital, Thompson excused himself. Paul frowned, but didn't say anything. His frown turned into a grin several minutes later when Thompson rejoined him and handed his chief a hot cup of coffee from the cafeteria.

"You read my mind," Paul exclaimed. Thompson grinned.

Going through the footage was tedious work. They had to view numerous frames before they found the section that corresponded with their arrival at the hospital.

"There. We're pulling in now." He pointed at the screen, seeing the two police cruisers pulling in and parking side by side. He watched as he got out and then walked around to let Irene out. She retrieved Mary Ann. They appeared to be talking. He couldn't even remember what they had been talking about.

They moved out of the camera view. A few minutes passed. Suddenly, Paul noticed movement in the trees.

"Look! On the right!" Was that him?

Yep. It sure was. A young man on a motorcycle flew across the road and swerved into the parking lot. In fluid movements, he was off the bike and removed his helmet before he set to work on Paul's car. There was no other movement on that side of the lot. They'd parked there to be away from others, little knowing that their perp would be bold enough to approach out in the open.

Within moments, Paul's lock had been jimmied open and the bomb was in place. This was no amateur. As Trevor had surmised, the man was a pro. This was very obviously not the first bomb he'd ever handled.

When he was finished, their bomber cleaned up all traces of his presence and hopped back on the bike. As he hefted his helmet in one hand, he looked straight at the camera and jerked his right arm up in an arrogant salute, the movement sharp and precise. He knew exactly where the camera was and that they would look for him afterward. He wanted Paul to know who had killed Irene. Paul couldn't hold back the shudder that rolled through him.

He wanted to close his eyes and forget about the scene replaying on the screen, though of course he couldn't. Irene was counting on him. He forced himself to focus.

"Go back to where he was looking at the camera," Paul ground out, fury boiling up inside him. He choked back the bile that was thick in his throat.

The screen froze on the man's face.

"Bingo." Paul narrowed his gaze at the image before him. In his mind, he was seeing a younger version of the same face, standing in the photograph beside Niko Carter. "I am going to find you and put you away for a long time, my friend. It's time you learned the meaning of justice."

Irene walked into her house and wanted to weep. Her mother walked out of the kitchen, wiping her hands on a dish towel, Izzy at her heels. Mary Ann squealed at the sight of the dog. Irene set her down, knowing that the dog would watch over her. The scent of her mother's meat loaf permeated the air.

Her mother made the best meat loaf.

"Mom, when did you get here?"

"Well, is that any way to greet your mother?" Vera smiled, taking the sting out of her words. "The boys were getting restless, so I brought them over."

Irene hugged her mom, holding on until she got her emotions under control.

"*Please* don't take this the wrong way, Mom. I am really happy to see you. And I can't wait to see the boys. But it's not safe for you to be here right now. Someone's after me. They planted a bomb in Paul's car."

Vera gasped, her wrinkled hand flying to cover her pearly lipsticked mouth. "Oh, no! Are you okay? You don't seem hurt. What about Paul? Was he injured?"

Irene placed a hand on her mother's shoulder. Troubled tears clouded the older woman's eyes. Irene understood. There was more than just fear in that look. Vera Tucker still mourned the daughter who had been killed twelve years before. She probably always would. Irene wasn't sure you could ever completely heal from something like that.

"Easy, Mom. Everyone's okay. Paul's not hurt and he will be here after he finishes collecting evidence."

"Mommy!"

The somber mood was dispelled as two whirlwinds swept into the room. Irene bent to embrace both of her sons, inhaling their little-boy scent. It brought with it its own form of comfort.

"Hey, guys. Were you good for Granny?"

"I was." Matthew poked a thumb into his chest. Then he turned it toward his brother. "Not him, though. He didn't wash his hands before he licked the bowl."

Irene listened to their chatter as they set the table and sat down to eat. She asked Parker to bring in the high chair stored in the garage. When asked if he wanted to join them for supper, he refused politely.

"Smells good, ma'am, but I'm on duty. It would be more than my life was worth if the chief thought I wasn't protecting you properly." He went back out to scan the perimeter again.

Irene blushed. Her mother flashed a satisfied grin her way.

"You can get those thoughts out of your mind, Mom. There's nothing going on between Paul and me."

Liar, her mind whispered. She ignored it.

"I didn't say anything. Although if anything were to develop between you two, there'd be nothing wrong with that. You've been alone for three years now. That's more than enough time to mourn. Now it's time for you to move on."

Move on. How did one do that?

After dinner, she helped her mother clean up the dinner dishes. There were leftovers. Although Irene protested, her mom insisted she keep them.

"It's only me at home," Vera reasoned. "I made enough for you and the boys to have another meal. And if I remember correctly, Paul enjoys my meat loaf, too."

Irene rolled her eyes, ignoring her mom's blatant matchmaking. If only her mom knew how impossible such a match would be. Irene didn't want to tell her mom how broken she was, though. It would only cause her more heartache. Her mom had enough tragedies in her past. She didn't need to add Irene's problems to her burdens.

Parker walked Vera out to her car and then returned to his watch. Irene was thankful for his presence, but worry still chewed at her mind, nibbling away her confidence bit by bit. The criminals after her had attacked her so many times, despite the protection around her. What was to keep them from coming through one policeman to get her?

Soft weeping caught her attention, distracting her from her concern for Parker. She quickly tracked the sound back to the crib in the bedroom, Izzy on her heels. Mary Ann was holding tight to one of Matthew's stuffed animals, his favorite crocodile. Hours earlier, Irene had watched as he'd handed it to her solemnly. Irene had swallowed tears at that one. Matthew loved that animal.

"She needs it more, Mommy. 'Cause she don't have her mommy here."

Her sweet boy. He made her so proud and broke her heart at the same time.

AJ had swung his arm around his little brother's shoulders when he noticed his brother's lip had started to quiver. "Come on, Matthew," AJ had said, very mature. "You can sleep with Bubba."

Matthew had perked up. Bubba was AJ's prized stuffed cow. No one got to touch Bubba.

"Really?"

A sniffle brought her back to the present. Lowering the side, Irene reached in and lifted the small girl from the bed. Her bonnet had been removed, and her braids swung free over her shoulders, wisps of brown hair escaping from them.

"It's all right, Mary Ann. I'm here." She kept her voice soft, placing a kiss on the child's forehead.

"Mam." Mary Ann sobbed, burying her face in Irene's shoulder. "Me *mam*."

Tears spurted from Irene's own eyes. "I know, baby. I know you want your *mam*. We'll get you home just as soon as we can." Sitting in the rocking chair, she slowly rocked the baby back to sleep.

As she was replacing her in the crib, her phone dinged.

Paul had sent a message. On my way soon.

Ok. Mom left meat loaf. She hit Send on the message.

A minute later there was another ping. This time she grinned at the message. I'm telling Thompson to use his siren. Your mom's meat loaf is the best.

Irene watched out the window, waiting for

him to arrive. She'd taken some Tylenol for the headache she felt coming on. The dull throb was just beginning to ebb when headlights turned into her driveway. Parker got up and joined the men at the car. She saw them chat for a few minutes before Parker waved and strode down to his own vehicle and left.

Thompson stayed in the car. Paul moved up to the door and knocked.

Irene became aware of Izzy pressing up against her side, fluffy tail slapping the ground with a thump-thump as she wagged it.

"I know, girl. I like him, too," Irene whispered, petting the dog's sleek head.

She opened the door and he stepped inside. More than anything she wanted him to pull her into his arms, the way he'd done earlier. But he didn't, and she wasn't about to make a move toward him. It wasn't like she really wanted him to hug her. She reminded herself that she had no room in her life for another cop. And he was apparently trying to keep his distance, as well.

But his face… It seemed to have aged since that morning. Weariness emanated from him. When had she ever seen Paul so tired, so drawn? The answer was never. He'd always seemed to have the energy and drive of ten men. Now he looked like he was ready to fall over.

"Hey, you look beat. Come into the kitchen and get some meat loaf."

He nodded, but had yet to say anything.

In the kitchen, she motioned for him to sit at the table. He complied, his movements weary. Now she was really concerned.

She set a plate of warm meat loaf and a baked potato before him and pulled a large frosted mug from the freezer. She filled it with milk and handed it to him. He tipped his head and drained most of the glass, setting it back on the table with an exaggerated "ah." Just like her kids did.

A laugh escaped her. "More?"

"Please. I needed that."

Finally, he spoke. She realized a grin was tugging at her lips and turned to hide it.

Soon, all inclination to grin faded. As he ate, Paul related what he'd found.

"It doesn't make sense. Isn't going after me in such a public way counterintuitive? Wouldn't the kidnappers want to be staying under the radar?"

Paul nodded. "This is more than a random reaction, Irene. I think that we have some sort of kidnapping organization here. I need to contact the surrounding precincts. Both to see if they can lend us some manpower, and to let them know of the possibility of a kidnapping ring. I think the man who planted that bomb has gone rogue. And I think he's ex-military."

The room tilted. She had been leaning against the counter. Now she stood upright abruptly.

"Which means he's someone with training."

"Yeah." Paul finished his meal and took his plate to the sink. "Tomorrow, I want to head into the station and see if I can find out who he is. Also, I need to find out as much info as I can about the new missing child and Mary Ann's family. Do you think you'd be ready to make a trip Wednesday morning to Ohio?"

She thought of something. "My boss has been really lenient about me taking time off. But I do need to go to the meeting tomorrow."

He tilted his head. "What meeting? I don't remember anything about a meeting."

"I had forgotten about it. But it's for the family I was visiting when I first saw the bearded man. Tomorrow at four." She waited anxiously.

His face grew fierce. "You're kidding, right? How on earth can you go to a meeting when all this is going on?"

Her own temper rose. "I don't want to lose my job! Others can handle the rest of the visits. I was brought on board after they were started. This case is all mine. No one else knows the family yet."

He scowled. "You're not going alone."

She opened her mouth. He shook his head. "No way, Irene. It's completely nuts, but I will let you go if I can go with you."

She huffed, but secretly was relieved. "I wasn't going to argue."

"One more thing. My cruiser is not in shape to be driven. We'll have to use your car."

She started to wash the dishes. The air crackled between them. Tension, attraction, or both? As much as she tried to deny it, she could feel something brewing between them. *Lord, help me to guard my heart.*

After drying her hands on the towel hanging on the stove, she turned to find him watching her. Her breath caught in her throat. There was so much tenderness, so much longing in that look, it robbed her of all thought. Then he straightened and the expression was gone. Had she imagined it?

"How about some coffee?" she asked, trying to ease the electric current between them.

He smiled. A slow, easy smile that made her pulse hike. "There's never a bad time for coffee."

She smiled back as she reached for the button on the Keurig.

"Irene, stop!" Paul's shout reached her a moment too late, just as she touched the machine. Sparks flew out in every direction. A jolt shot through her fingertips at the same moment that Paul grabbed the broom from the corner and swept the machine from the countertop and into the empty sink.

Paul grabbed the fire extinguisher off the wall and used it to douse the smoking coffee maker.

For the second time that day, she'd escaped death because of Paul's quick thinking. She knew in her bones this was no accident. Just as she knew the person responsible wouldn't give up. What she didn't know was if she'd survive the next time.

ELEVEN

Irene sat, dazed, as the smell of smoke filled the air. The smoke detector let out four shrill beeps before Paul yanked it off the wall, silencing it. Then Paul rushed to her side and called to her. She felt his warm hand on her shoulder as he gently shook her.

"Irene? Irene! Come on, Red. Can you hear me? Are you okay?"

She turned her head, stunned, and stared into his concerned gaze. "I'm fine. My hand feels funny, but the numbness is already fading." She looked down at her shocked hand, amazed to find it looked completely normal. It felt like the tips of her fingers had been singed off.

She took in the countertop. The foam from the fire extinguisher had started to dissipate, but she could tell it would leave a mess behind it. The Keurig was damaged beyond repair. It had never had problems before. The machine was only three months old. Jace and Melanie had given it to her on her last birthday.

"That was no accident." Her words were not a question. They left a bitter taste on her tongue. Fury and anguish battled for control. Not from the incident itself. No, her feeling of helpless anger was more due to the fact that someone had violated her home, had come into her personal space and tried to do her and her family harm. That was the final straw for her.

"I know." Paul surveyed the machine grimly. "Which means that our guy knows you survived his earlier attempt. The fact that he was bold enough to come and sabotage this machine terrifies me, Irene. I don't have enough manpower to watch your house when you're not here. And I'm afraid he'll go after your family to get to you."

She froze. Her boys. Paul was right. The wacko coming after her was vicious enough to use her children against her.

"What do I do?" Was that wobbly voice hers? She sounded like she was all of ten years old. Honestly, she couldn't take any more. *Lord, why? I'm trying to trust You again, but this doesn't make it easy.* Even as she cried out to her God, she knew she had enough faith to continue to trust and believe.

Paul paced, rubbing his hand across his chin

as he considered his options. Finally, he nodded. "Your mom…her house is protected with a security system, right?"

She sat up. "Yes. She had it put in several years ago, when someone was after Melanie."

He stopped pacing and faced her, shoving his hands in his back pockets. "Yeah, I remember that. Irene, I think you should call your mom. Let her know you, the boys and Mary Ann are coming and why. I don't want her to be taken off guard. There will be continued police protection, but the security system will alert us to any intruders or issues during the day when no one is home. And if I remember right, the retired fire chief is across the street. He knows the drill. Shouldn't mind keeping an eye on the place."

Irene didn't even hesitate. She called her mom, who immediately agreed. Irene hated bringing her problems home to her mother's door, but knew it was necessary to protect them all. Paul had gone outside to let Thompson in on what had happened. By the time Irene had woken the boys, the two cops had reviewed the kitchen scene and confirmed that the coffee maker had been tampered with.

She heard Thompson mutter, "This dude is either brave or stupid, Chief, messing with your coffee."

"You got that right," Paul replied, his familiar drawl back in place.

Shaking her head, Irene went to hurry the boys along.

"We can take Izzy, right, Mom?" Matthew asked, his lower lip pushed out in a slight pout.

"Of course, buddy. Izzy's family." She tousled his hair.

"What about the girls?" AJ queried, pushing his glasses up on his little nose.

Oh, boy. That one wasn't going to go over well with her mom. The "girls" were Jelly Bean and Oreo, a couple of rats the boys had gotten from Jace last year. Irene hadn't been pleased. Their grandmother had pitched a fit when she'd seen them. But if they stayed here, who knew when they'd get back? And she wasn't about to return twice a day to feed them. She made an executive decision.

"Get their food together, and we'll take them. Make sure you have everything they'll need for several days."

She monitored the boys packing for a few minutes before hurrying to pack for herself and Mary Ann. Within an hour, they were ready to go.

Irene opened the hatchback and whistled. Izzy hopped up inside. Irene couldn't help remembering that only a few days ago they'd opened the door to find Mary Ann hidden inside. Shivering, she shut the door and climbed into the driver's seat. Should she have let Paul drive?

He was looking comfortable in the passenger seat. She had never thought of asking. She glanced back at the seat behind them. Her sons were situated on either side of Mary Ann, taking turns making her laugh. The rats were safely in their cage on the floor at AJ's feet.

The moment she backed out of the driveway and started down the road, Thompson pulled away from the curb and followed her. The plan was that he would give Paul a ride home once she and the children were situated.

It was a testament to how serious the situation was that her mother saw the rat cage coming into her house and didn't say anything. Her complexion turned a little green, and one slender, blue-veined hand pressed her mouth as if she were feeling ill. Still, she didn't protest.

"Sorry, Mom." Irene muttered, guilt swamping her.

"Never you mind, Irene. We'll do whatever we need to. All that matters is that you and the kids stay safe."

That was the end of the conversation. The rats were soon safely tucked away in the boys' usual room. The room that had once belonged to her sister, she reflected.

Paul didn't stay inside long after they arrived. He and Thompson did a thorough check of the house and grounds to make sure everything was safe and that the security system was working well. Irene knew a cruiser would be parked outside all night.

Paul himself would be going home. She was embarrassed to realize how much she didn't want him to leave. But she knew it was best. He didn't have a vehicle here, and he really needed some sleep. He looked like he wanted to say something.

"What?" she asked.

He sighed, a sound of pure frustration. "Oh, nothing that won't keep."

She knew him better than that. Whatever he wanted to tell her, it was important. At least to him. Although she doubted it had anything to do with her safety. If it did, he would have said it, whether her mom was within listening distance or not.

Well, whatever it was, it didn't matter now. He had gone home, and she was safe inside here. It was better this way.

But even as she shut the door behind him, she had to ignore the sense of loneliness that swept in.

* * *

All he wanted was a cup of coffee. Paul made his way out to the office coffee station and poured some in his favorite travel mug. It was hot. That was good. Already his morning was looking brighter. He took a tentative sip. Ugh. He made a gagging face at Lieutenant Dan Willis, who smirked back at him.

"Sorry, Chief. Parker made the coffee."

He just knew that Dan was laughing at him, which was cruel. He lifted his mug in Dan's direction. "This is not coffee. I think it might be watered-down diesel fuel."

Parker sauntered in. "Anything to get your engine running."

"Oh, man," Paul groaned. "Bad coffee and terrible jokes. What did I do to deserve this?"

Both officers chuckled.

A few minutes later, Dan was all business. "Sir? I think you need to see this."

Paul's stomach tightened. It was either really good news or really bad. Dan moved over so he could get a look at the information on his monitor. Paul whistled quietly. Gazing back at them from the computer screen was the image of a young man in a US Army uniform. Private William Sharps, EOD specialist. Dishonorable discharge.

There was a string of minor complaints. He

had done a year in prison around two years ago. And he had been ordered by a judge to undergo counseling after assaulting a girlfriend, something he never completed.

Paul scanned the information. One comment stuck out. His commanding officer had said he was "a brilliant young man with a short fuse and a profound lack of empathy. He seems to enjoy other people's pain."

Not a good thing to find in a soldier. And definitely not a person you'd want chasing you. Yet that was the man who had it in for Irene. Why? Paul was still working on that one, although he believed that Carter's death was the event that tipped Sharps over the edge.

"Lieutenant Willis," he addressed Dan, "please see that this information is sent to all surrounding precincts. This man is dangerous, and is responsible for at least two attempted murders. Oh, and he is highly skilled at setting off explosives, so caution is advised."

Dan nodded and stood. Paul knew his officers. Dan was the model of efficiency. Paul could trust that his orders would be carried out to the letter and that Dan would advise him of any responses or changes in quick order.

His next plan of action was to track down Mary Ann's family. After a half hour, he was more than frustrated. Lapp was an extremely popular name in that particular part of the country.

He began to check with the local police in the area to find out if there were any fires involving Amish families where a young child with Down syndrome was supposedly killed. That turned out to be quite a project. There were three departments in cities within the county and five police departments from counties near enough to have been involved.

He spent the better part of the morning and his entire lunch hour on the phone chasing down leads. He came away with nothing. His frustration grew. Irene needed him to solve this fast. Her very life depended upon it. What a time for Jace and Miles to be out of the area at a trial. He could have really used them about now.

Finally, his diligence paid off. There had been four suspicious fires in the past two weeks throughout the region. Three of them involved Amish in some way. As to casualties, that was a little confusion. Two or more of them seemed to have resulted in at least one death. But that was all gossip. There were no coroner reports, only local talk. At least two of them seemed to be connected to the name Lapp, but even that was unclear. Still, it was more than he'd had an hour ago.

Paul caught sight of the clock on the wall and exclaimed in dismay. It was two thirty. He'd promised Irene he'd arrive no later than three fifteen so she'd be at the meeting on time.

He worked feverishly for the next half hour before calling it a day. Parker would give him a ride out to Vera's house so Parker could spell Jackson on watch duty.

No sooner had he arrived than Irene ran out the door, red laptop bag over her shoulder and two travel mugs in her hand. Two? He grinned as he stepped from Parker's cruiser and was handed a travel mug.

"Dan called and said your coffee at the station was below par this morning," she announced by way of greeting.

"Hey!" Parker mock-glowered at her. "I do my best."

"Sorry." She didn't look apologetic. Smug, yes. Sorry, no. "At least you're a good cop. That's the important thing."

Parker grinned.

"You ready to move out?" *Silly question, Kennedy. She's here with her bag, isn't she?*

"Yeah. The sooner this meeting is over, the better I'll feel about it. I get the willies just thinking of going near that place."

Who wouldn't? Paul kept that thought to himself, not wanting to dampen her high spirits.

She'd had enough put on her shoulders in the past few days to make anyone depressed. This upbeat Irene was the Irene he used to know.

He was pretty sure some of the cheer was forced. That was fine, too. She was brave and trying to keep a positive outlook. In a way, so was he.

He got into her SUV with her and buckled himself in. Glancing up, he caught the tender look in her eyes before she shifted her gaze. Did she have feelings for him, too? The brief surge of hope was drowned out by the knowledge that he couldn't allow her to become attached to him.

Soon, very soon, he'd have to talk with her about his past. So she would know why this relationship developing between them could never go anywhere. He'd feel pretty ridiculous if she said that she was sorry, but the feelings were all on his side. Though maybe that would be preferable. The last thing he wanted was to break her heart.

His was another story. He had the feeling it was too late for him.

Pull yourself together, Kennedy. These maudlin thoughts will get you nowhere.

Pulling himself straighter in his seat, he spent the rest of the ride to the Zilchers' house filling her in on what he'd learned that day.

He'd been tempted to wait, but felt that would be unfair. She deserved to know. To his relief, she seemed to take it all in stride.

"So you were right. About Sharps being military, I mean," she mused. "I didn't think he'd pick up knowledge about explosives and that sort of thing off the street."

She flipped on the blinker and turned onto the street where the Zilchers lived. All conversation died. Her posture grew taut. He could see her slim fingers clench on the wheel. She pulled into the driveway behind the other cars and put the car in Park, yet made no move to get out. Her gaze shifted toward the other house. The crime-scene tape was still up. The blinds were shut.

Paul leaned over and covered her hand with his. She jumped, then snorted.

"I can't believe I'm being this stupid."

"Hey." He caught her chin in his hand and turned her face to his. The glimmer of tears in her eyes was almost his undoing. Man, he wished he had the right to take her in his arms and kiss those tears away. Or the ability to tell her with absolute certainty that everything would be fine. He did what he could. "Irene, you're not being stupid. You have been so brave, so strong, these past few days, I am filled with admiration for you. And you are not alone here. I will be with you the entire time."

She nodded, throwing her shoulders back and lifting her chin. "Right. Let's do this." She turned to open the door, then cut a shy glance back at him. "Thanks. It means a lot that you're here."

"Who else will be inside?"

She stopped and tilted her head to consider, then ticked off the participants on her fingers. Altogether, there would be four other people besides them and the family at the table. He relaxed. That many people made it highly unlikely that Sharps would attack here. He told her so.

"Still, you have your gun, right?"

He grinned at the question and patted the service weapon in its holster. "Right here."

"Then we're good. Let's go."

They exited the vehicle together.

The meeting went smoothly. The parents and other educators were initially intimidated by the presence of an armed police officer. But after a few minutes the meeting grew so intense that they forgot about him.

About forty minutes into the meeting, Paul excused himself to the kitchen when Dan called. He listened as his lieutenant explained that they had managed to find the link between

Sharps and Carter. Turned out the two were second cousins and had grown up together. The best they could figure out was that one of them had recruited the other to the kidnapping ring.

Five minutes later, Paul could hear that the meeting was breaking up. He peered through the doorway and his blood ran cold. The seat where Irene had sat just a few minutes ago was empty.

"Gotta go." He hung up as he dashed through the door. The startled team members stared at him, mouths wide-open. He didn't care. "Where's Irene?"

His voice came out hard. Almost angry.

"Our meeting is done. She needed to make a call to her office. I think she went out to the back porch."

Paul tore through the house to the porch. No Irene. Her phone was lying on the wooden deck. He picked the phone up and then turned to scan in all directions. Something caught his attention. Was that movement in the abandoned house? It was too shadowy to know for sure— the blinds were still down—but his instinct was screaming at him that Irene was there. And not by herself.

He called Dan back. "Irene's gone. I think the perp has taken her to the crime-scene house.

I'm going in. No time to wait for backup, so get here quick."

He disconnected before Dan could answer, already moving toward the house. He had no idea what he would find. But he knew that if he needed to put himself in front of a bullet to save Irene, he wouldn't even hesitate.

TWELVE

Irene struggled to break free as she was dragged through the line of trees to the house that would haunt her forever. One of Black Beard's meaty hands was across her mouth and nose. If she started to lag, he tightened his grip and she suddenly found herself unable to breathe. She had no choice but to keep up with the brutal man. Branches scraped her face, abusing her tender skin. A trickle dripped down her cheek. She was bleeding.

At the back door to his former house, he thrust her inside. She noted that the crime-scene tape had been cut. She saw only darkness for a minute or two until her eyes began to adjust to the dim light.

Black Beard kicked the door behind him shut. The sound was so final that Irene cringed. The imagery of a casket lid being shut flashed into her mind. She waggled her head as much as the man's hold would allow to dislodge the image. Such thoughts would only serve to keep her locked in fear, unable to act. She refused to be a victim.

A human-sized shadow moved toward them until Irene was finally able to see the woman who stood before her. It took her a moment, but then her eyes flared wide as recognition sent shock waves through her.

The woman she'd been so concerned about less than a week ago stood before her. Except now there was no sign of an Amish bonnet. Of Amish anything. This woman was completely Englisch, from her skinny jeans and oversize sweater to her edgy haircut, heavy eye makeup and double pierced ears. The young woman shook her head when she saw Irene. Her shoulders slumped. She was the picture of dejection.

"Oh, Eddie," she whispered. "Why would you go and do something this stupid?"

Eddie? This monster holding her had an ordinary, pleasant name like "Eddie"?

"I don't want to hear it, Brenda." Irene shivered at the angry growl so close to her ears.

"Well, you're gonna hear about it. We coulda got the money Billy stashed and ran. He said to meet him, not go grabbing anyone else."

"Billy! I'm sick of listening to Billy. He's gonna get us all caught the way he's been chasing after this one. And for what? Because his cousin went and got himself killed. I say, we get rid of her, then there's no one left who can identify us. And then he'll have to start playing by the rules again. We can start over again in another state."

Brenda crossed her arms and glared.

Irene held her breath. She was getting an awful lot of information here. Which meant that neither of them expected her to live to share it with the authorities. But, surely, Paul had to be looking for her.

Brenda started talking. "I'm done, Eddie Dillinger. You can take your money and leave. I ain't never gonna put on another of those dresses and bonnets again."

"You're as much of a pain as your loser boyfriend was. I don't need you."

Without warning, Eddie reached into his coat pocket and brought out a gun. Brenda had time to open her mouth, gaping like a fish, before he pulled the trigger. She screamed and grabbed her stomach before falling to the floor, crying in pain.

"And now, it's time I took care of you," he said to Irene, his acrid breath fanning across her face as he pushed his face against the side of hers. She struggled not to gag.

Before he could lift the gun again, it was shot out of his hand. Irene found herself suddenly free as the big man howled and cradled his injured hand.

Paul stepped into the room, his expression tight and grim. He advanced slowly, his service weapon never wavering off the man.

"I called for backup. They should be here within five minutes."

It was actually only four minutes until backup arrived, and they were followed closely by an ambulance. Irene hadn't been harmed, no doubt thanks to Paul's quick intervention. And God's protection. She may have doubted in the past, but now she was sure He was looking after her. How else would she have survived all this?

Physically, she was fine. Emotionally, though, she was starting to feel wrung out. As for the two kidnappers, they both needed treatment. It would be touch and go with the woman named Brenda. She'd taken a hit to her abdomen. Even as Irene watched from the sidelines, Brenda kept fading in and out of consciousness. Eddie, however, would definitely live to stand trial. He was handcuffed, both hands in front, his injured hand bandaged. He was also yelling angrily at everyone he looked at. Irene cringed at the foul language coming out of his mouth.

Eddie caught her watching him. A sneer curled his lip under the thick beard. She could see his teeth. The sudden thought struck her that he could be considered an attractive man, but one hardly noticed because of the anger and cruelty emanating from him.

"You ain't safe yet, pretty girl." Eddie spit in her direction. "Billy'll hunt you down and gut you like a deer. It's only a matter of time."

Paul stepped into the room, "That's enough."

His voice was harder than Irene had ever heard it. She started at the sound of it. She wasn't the only one. The man who'd been throwing threats and insults her way seconds ago subsided, although he continued to glower as one of the police officers lead him away.

Irene couldn't remember ever seeing Paul this angry, either. Paul didn't get angry. He was so calm nothing ever ruffled his feathers or got the better of him. *Except when I'm in trouble.*

Not ready to deal with that thought yet, Irene continued to watch as Brenda was loaded onto a stretcher and wheeled out the door. She really hoped the girl would survive. It would mean she would go to jail, yes, but even in jail, one could find redemption. The Lord could work anywhere, she was beginning to understand.

Quietly, she murmured a prayer for the woman's healing and conversion.

"Amen."

Irene nearly jumped out of her skin at Paul's

deep voice so close to her ear. She had been so preoccupied with Brenda's situation she hadn't paid any attention to where Paul was in the room. Not that she'd forgotten about him. She knew he was there. And felt safer because of it.

"Can I ask you why you didn't let me know where you were going before heading to the back porch alone?"

Was he mad at her? He didn't sound mad. Just calm. Which meant nothing.

She gazed into his eyes and breathed a sigh of relief. What she saw there was warmth and concern. He had been worried, she knew that.

"I wasn't planning on leaving the house." She felt inclined to defend herself. "I just needed a little privacy to make a call. The house next door was still abandoned, or so I had thought. There were no vehicles in the driveway, no hint that anyone was there. I was done with my call and had turned to return inside when he grabbed me from behind and yanked me down the steps."

Paul brushed a hand down the side of her head. "Your brother would have my head if I let anything happen to you."

She stiffened at the thought that his concern for her was all due to his friendship with Jace.

Then he touched her chin, turning her head

to look at him again. "And I would have been pretty upset myself."

Softening, she leaned into the hand on her face. What was she doing? She didn't want to encourage his affections...did she? She was growing more confused by the moment. To regain her equilibrium, she took a step away and laughed shakily.

"I'll try not to get into trouble again."

Paul frowned, but let her go. "Do that. In the meantime, are you finished with the meeting? Can we go? I want to be at the hospital when that woman comes out of surgery."

Good grief. She had completely forgotten about her clients.

"Almost done. I am so happy that I'm the service coordinator and not a therapist. Sweet kid, I just don't think I could go back there every week. I do need to collect my things. Then we can go."

It was funny how life went on around you even when your world was being torn upside down.

Before heading to the hospital, Paul drove Irene back to her mother's house so she could change. Every house on her mother's block was in full Christmas mode. Which was not surprising, as they were just over three weeks out. Mrs. Tucker's house was ablaze with lights and a lavishly decorated tree sat in the front window. She even had the two evergreens in the front yard decked out.

Man, he hadn't decorated for Christmas for years. It hadn't made sense, him being a bachelor and all. He celebrated his Savior every day in his heart. The decorations wouldn't change that. No, that seemed like something a family would do. A family he'd always assumed he'd never have.

But now he was starting to want a family.

Correction. He wanted Irene's family. He wanted to see *her* smiling at him every day, not some random woman his matchmaking mother or sister claimed would make a good wife. Because as much as he denied it, he knew that the feelings he'd once had for the teenage Irene were growing again. Only stronger and deeper.

He had to find William Sharps. Once the threat to Irene was gone, he could move on. Either with or without her. He'd seen her withdrawal earlier. She obviously had misgivings about getting closer to him.

Well, who wouldn't? Especially given their past together. And she didn't know the worst about him. Not yet. But he was determined that she would. Tonight. He'd tell her tonight.

But not now. Right now, they needed to go to the hospital. He knew he could leave her here at her mother's house. Zee had been approved to return to work, so he had her watching the school AJ and Matthew attended. They were home now. Parker was coming to take over the watch. And some of the other officers had dropped off a new cruiser for him to use while his was being fixed up. He wouldn't leave her, though. He didn't care what anyone thought. He was taking no more chances with Irene. Or her family.

Irene walked out the front door and took his breath away. Her gorgeous red hair was hidden under a warm wool hat, but it didn't matter. She still looked just as beautiful as she was, inside and out. She was strong and confident, and he sensed her newly rediscovered relationship with God had brought her some peace. She glowed with it. And his heart ached.

In each hand, she held a new travel mug. Exactly what his tired brain needed. Caffeine.

Paul jumped out of his side to walk around to her door and open it. It was the gentlemanly thing to do. And it got him his coffee faster. She handed him his mug as she folded herself neatly into her seat. It smelled wonderful.

"Thanks for the coffee." He slid into his seat and fastened his belt. "It's not anything fancy, right? Not like the tutti-frutti stuff you like."

"Please—" she added an extra flair to her

eye-roll "—I know you better than that, Paul Kennedy. Yours is black, and way too strong for my liking. And mine's not fancy. It's just coffee with English toffee creamer. You should try it. It's yummy."

"Yeah, no thanks."

Still, he chuckled at the face she made.

Then it was down to business. He couldn't let himself get distracted before the case was fully closed. There was too much of a risk that she'd be attacked again.

At the hospital, they were directed to wait. And wait.

Finally, they were given the word that Brenda had survived the surgery. They waited a couple more hours before they were allowed to go in. It was almost nine. Visiting hours had ended. Paul had bought them both something to eat from the cafeteria although neither felt much like eating.

They entered the ultrasterile room together. Paul had instructed that Brenda be put in a private room with a guard at all times. The less contact she had with any of the other patients, the better. Irene situated herself in a chair near the wall. Paul moved to stand at the side of her bed.

Brenda's eyelids fluttered open about three-quarters of the way. She still looked drowsy from the anesthesia. When she saw Paul in his uniform, a gentle sigh left her.

"Knew you'd come see me," she mumbled, her voice thick. "Eddie dead?"

"No, ma'am. Eddie's been arrested for kidnapping and at least one murder and another attempted murder."

"He killed the paramedic," she said tonelessly. "And I think he would have killed the redhead if you hadn't interrupted him."

"And he tried to kill you, too. As for the kidnapping, you will be under arrest when you leave here." He recited her rights. She nodded her understanding. "I need you to tell me about the kidnapping operation. Is there another child you've kidnapped recently?"

He expected resistance, but Brenda had apparently given up.

"We had to take another kid to replace the one you cops are protecting. Folks already paid half for her. Got her from an Amish family in Indiana. We were supposed to go to the new safe house and meet up with Billy before delivering her to her new family. When we didn't show up, Billy probably took her and collected the rest of the money himself."

She gave up the address for the new parents without demur when asked.

"Why were you back at the house?"

Her lids fluttered shut again. He was afraid she'd fallen asleep. She answered though, much to his relief. "Had to leave quickly last week. Turns out Billy left money there that we didn't know about. He was out that day. Didn't know we'd left it behind till later."

"Who put the little girl in the SUV?"

Irene tensed. He heard her chair creak as she leaned forward.

"I did." Her eyes opened again, and she looked past him to Irene. "I saw your face when you came to the house. You looked so nice. Eddie was angry at me. I had kidnapped the kid, but didn't know she had Down syndrome. Eddie saw her face and he flew off the handle. Said no one would want her. Hit me. I fell and cut my head." Now that she said it, he could see the scabbed cut on the side of her head. That explained the blood they'd found on Mary Ann. And on the floor. "I knew he would kill her if the family said they wouldn't take her."

Irene paled.

"Then why did he go after her and try to kidnap her again?" He could see her energy was fading, but he needed the answers while she was willing to give them.

"He thought it would be easier to get her than to try and find a new child in another Amish community. When he couldn't grab her, Billy said there was no choice but to find someone else. But that the redhead still had seen too much."

Irene.

"What was your role in the operation?"

"I'm so tired," she mumbled.

"You can sleep when you answer."

A tear slipped down her wan cheek. "The guys would cause some kind of accident—usually a fire. Always in some out-of-the-way community. That way it was unlikely fire inspectors and coroners would be involved. While everyone was running around trying to put the fire out, I would go in and find the youngest child. I dressed in Amish clothing, so no one would pay attention to me. I could walk in and walk out with the kid. But after Niko died, I was done. I shouldn't have ever agreed to it, and will feel guilty until I die."

"Why'd you agree to it?" Irene asked from her chair. She got up and walked over to stare down at the woman on the bed. There was pity in her gaze. But also anger and accusation. Paul knew he should be mad at her for interfering with his interrogation. But, in his mind, she had earned a right to ask the question.

"I didn't want to." Brenda kept her eyes closed. "But my guy, Niko, said if we didn't get the money, we'd never be able to marry and have a life together. Now he's gone, and nothing matters anymore."

"How many children have you taken?" Paul barked.

"Not that many. Eight. Maybe ten. Hard to remember. The one I put in your car was from Ohio. I don't remember exactly where. Somewhere in Holmes County."

It confirmed their information.

"What about the new child? Where is she from?"

"Oh, I remember that one very clearly. Mostly because I had already decided to get out of it and turn Eddie in." She rattled off an address in Indiana.

A minute later, the nurse came in and shooed them out.

It was a somber duo who returned to the Tucker house that evening. They didn't talk as they went inside. Vera had left the coffeepot on. Irene poured Paul a cup, then started to make herself a pot of tea.

"Why do people do it, Paul?"

Huh?

"What, Red? Why do people do what?" He took a long swallow of coffee. At this rate, he'd be up until three in the morning.

"Why do people make such dumb choices? That day when Eddie came chasing after me with the gun…if Brenda and Niko had just walked away, he'd be alive and she wouldn't be on her way to prison. They'd be poor, sure, but at least they'd have a chance."

This was the opening he needed to tell her. Nervousness settled over him. He couldn't shake it off.

"Well, Irene. Many people make really dumb choices. I've made some myself." She turned to face him. He wished she wouldn't. Looking at her face as he confessed his failings would be hard. But he was a man of honor now, and he wouldn't back down. "You remember that night when I left you behind at the dance?"

Yeah, she remembered. He saw the way her mouth tightened. But she didn't back away.

"You were the best thing in my life, Irene. You and Jace. But there were things about me you didn't know. That I couldn't tell you. I know you wondered why I never invited you to my house, to meet my parents." She nodded. "Well, I was ashamed. See, my mom, she's great. But my dad, well…"

He stood and paced to the door leading outside. *Give me strength, Lord.* "My dad had issues. Bad ones. Back then, he'd lost his job and become discouraged. Turned to alcohol. And later to drugs. He ended up in prison for vehicular homicide while driving drunk. And he died there."

Facing her, he saw the compassion in her eyes. That would change when she heard the rest. "You'd think I would have learned, right? I was so ashamed of what he'd done, but when I was fourteen, I started to get into his alcohol stash." Yeah, she saw where this was headed. He saw her grow pale. "I hid it for years, but I was an alcoholic by the time I was sixteen."

He couldn't face her and turned away. "I knew you were special. From the first time I saw you, I knew it. And I knew I wasn't worthy of you. Then your sister died, and you needed me to be someone you could lean on. I couldn't stand to see you in pain. That night, though, well, some of the other kids had snuck alcohol into the dance. And I didn't turn away from the temptation. I was pretty drunk, but still lucid enough, when one of the guys asked how my girlfriend would react seeing me drunk after her sister died because of drugs."

A soft sob sounded behind him. He flinched. "I had never been as ashamed of my father as I was of myself in that moment. I wasn't worthy of you. And never would be. I knew you'd be safe, that your friends would make sure you got home, so I walked out and didn't look back. I wasn't going to make you see me like that—

I wasn't going to put you anywhere near me while I was so out of control." He'd hated leaving her behind, even then. But he'd known it was the right thing to do. Then and now, she deserved so much better than him.

"I never touched a drop of alcohol after that. Not once in all these years. And Jace helped me reconcile with God. Then we moved, and I started over."

Footsteps. She walked over and joined him at the door. Put a hand on his arm. He didn't turn to look at her, just bowed his head and finished his story. "I moved back years later, and you had moved on. I was happy for you, Irene. I really was. Tony was a great man, an honest cop and a good friend. He made you as happy as you deserve to be—something that I could never do. I can't ever let down my guard. I was weak once. I refuse to let that happen again."

There was nothing more to be said. He set his cup in the dishwasher and left, knowing that between the security system and the cop on duty, she would be fine until morning. Which gave him time to get his head back in the game.

THIRTEEN

Paul picked up Irene at the assigned time. Mary Ann was remaining at her mother's house this time. Sergeant Zee was there with her, and another officer was keeping watch on the outside. Today, they were searching for the other child.

Irene had tried to talk at first—regular chit-chat, probably intended to get them back to normal—but he had given her short answers, so now they drove in silence. He tried to tell himself he was fine with the divide growing between them, but he wasn't. It was unbelievable how much you could miss someone when they were sitting right next to you.

Deliberately, he turned on the radio. More to drown out his own thoughts than anything else. He was amazed that she didn't seem to be disgusted with him after what he'd told her. How could she not be?

He came to a stop at a red light.

Jace never judged you. Why should she?

He blinked, momentarily dazzled by the epiphany. An epiphany cut short by a small beep from the car behind them. Oops. The light was green. It must have been green for a while for someone to honk their horn at a police car.

"I can't believe someone just honked at you!" Irene exclaimed, surprised out of her silence. Feeling a bit lighter, he chuckled and rolled down the window to wave at the annoyed driver.

"Nah. I was woolgathering when I should have been paying closer attention. Besides, it's not like they whaled on the horn. It was a polite beep."

He grinned at her snort, much happier than he'd been an hour ago.

Two hours later, they arrived at their destination—a large two-story brick house just outside of Pittsburgh, currently housing an Amish child who'd been stolen from her family. There were two cars in the drive, which had been meticulously shoveled. The house was completely decked out for Christmas, even more than Mrs. Tucker's. There was even a plastic sleigh on the roof.

"I hate that we're going to break their hearts." Although Irene wasn't facing him, the sadness in her voice was clear. He covered her hand with his, resealing the connection he'd almost destroyed.

"I don't want to sound cruel, Irene, but the truth is that we have to. Somewhere, there's a mother and father mourning for their daughter."

She nodded. When she finally faced him, her blue eyes were clear. "Thanks for letting me come."

"You kidding me? Like I'd leave you unguarded again. Uh-uh. You're stuck with me until this man gunning for you is put behind bars."

She flashed a smile his way. "Thanks, Paul. Okay. Let's go do this thing."

It was a hard visit. The parents were belligerent at first. They called their lawyer, who told them to do nothing until she arrived. So they were stuck waiting until she did. The animosity seething from the new parents was almost tangible. The little girl, however, was delightful—from the little they saw of her.

"How old do you think she is," Paul whispered to Irene when the woman left the room to take the little girl upstairs for a nap. To Paul's thinking, the kid hadn't looked in the least sleepy. Most likely, her new parents wanted to get her away from them. Couldn't blame them. Unfortunately, it wouldn't help.

"She's not much more than a year," Irene

whispered back. "Not much language yet, and she's still not quite walking steady."

The man sitting across from them glared, and they lapsed into silence.

Finally, the lawyer arrived. The first thing she did was question Irene's presence. Paul had already thought that one through.

"Irene is a special-education teacher trained to interact with emotionally fragile children— and we had reason to believe that might be the case here. The child that the kidnapping organization had originally planned to sell to your clients had been treated so harshly by men that only women were able to get near her." All true.

The mother's eyes grew wide with horror. "There was another child? What do you mean?"

Despite the pang of sympathy that struck him, he did his job.

"They kidnapped another girl, but didn't realize until afterward that she had Down syndrome. They didn't want to chance you backing out and demanding your money be returned. They stole the baby upstairs from Indiana, leaving her parents to think she'd been killed."

The look the woman gave her husband said it all. She wouldn't have accepted Mary Ann. Paul tightened his lips, holding his anger inside.

At that point, the lawyer demanded to see the couple's paperwork. Paul raised his eyebrows. He suspected that the couple had done the "adoption" without the lawyer. Her frown grew deeper as she read. The adoptive parents must have been able to gauge her expression because they were ashen by the time she looked up. "Christine. Jim. I am so sorry. None of these papers would hold up in court. They are a complete mockery. I wish you had consulted me before you started the adoption process."

He had been right. Not that there was any joy in it.

"But she is still ours, right?" Christine demanded. "We paid them ten thousand dollars. Doesn't that count for anything?"

Some of his sympathy vanished. "It doesn't matter how much you paid for her," Paul cut in. "The child was kidnapped from her real parents."

Her face grew red. "I don't mean to be unfeeling toward her birth parents. I really don't. But they already think she's dead. Please, we love her. She's our heart now."

"Christine." The lawyer's voice was unyielding. "You need to go get the child now. She is not yours, and if you don't give her up, the police are well within their rights to charge you with conspiracy to kidnap."

That finally got through to the weeping couple. Paul and Irene stood by grimly while they woke the child, crying over her. The wife held on tight at the last moment. Her husband eased the child out of her resisting arms and handed the baby to Irene. He caught his wife as she collapsed, sobbing.

"You need to go now," he ordered.

Paul held Irene's elbow as she carried the baby to the car. The little girl cried as she was buckled into the car seat. Irene sat in back with her to try to comfort the child as best as she could. What a rough few days the little one had been through.

Fortunately, they didn't have to go all the way back to Indiana to return her. Brenda had given them the family's name and address and Paul had sent two officers to Indiana to fetch the parents. They had left the night before. Sergeant Jackson had sent him a text saying they were on their way back earlier that morning. By the time they arrived at the station, they were already there.

Paul led Irene and the girl into the station. A sudden cry rent the room. "Edith!"

The baby in Irene's arms wiggled like a worm, desperate to get down. The moment Irene set her down, she was off, running on unsteady legs into her *mam*'s arms. The little family huddled close together, speaking in Pennsylvania Dutch together as if they were alone.

Paul noticed that the officers all had silly, sappy smiles on their faces. He had started to shake his head when he realized he was grinning, too. Irene wasn't just smiling. She was radiant at the sight of the parents being reunited with their child.

"Danke. Danke," the parents said to him and Irene as they made to go home with their child. "We thought our Edith was dead. Gott has blessed us. Our daughter is alive. *Danke* for finding her."

One family reunited. One to go.

And one killer still on the loose.

Joy was amazing. It energized you and wore you out at the same time.

Irene slipped into bed that night so exhausted she was sure she'd never get to sleep. But soon she was nodding off. That's when the nightmares came. Nightmares of men with black beards chasing her. Strangers wearing hooded sweatshirts shooting at her. Walking into the kitchen and her mother telling her someone had kidnapped the boys as she cooked pancakes for breakfast.

Irene woke up, fear pumping through her blood, the urge to run still fighting with reality.

The children are safe. There is a police officer right outside. She checked on her boys and

Mary Ann anyway. They were all three snug in their beds, asleep.

What to do now? Going back to bed was out of the question. As much as she needed more sleep, she dreaded the prospect of another nightmare.

The unsettled feeling continued as she went to the kitchen to fix herself a cup of tea, hoping it might settle her down. She filled the kettle and put it on the stove. While she was waiting, she let her thoughts wonder. Over Mary Ann. Her boys. Paul. What was she feeling toward him? And how was he feeling toward her? She reviewed his story about his past. It didn't bother her as much as he'd expected it to, that was clear. The thing was, she knew that people had weaknesses. And she also knew Paul. His strength. His dedication. He was an honest man who had fallen once. Of course, she could forgive him for that. But forgiving him wasn't the same as trusting him with her heart. He was still a cop—was that an obstacle she'd ever be able to overcome?

As she pondered, her gaze fell on her mother's well-worn Bible.

When had she last read the Word of God? Contrition touched her heart. *Sorry, Lord.*

Pulling the book off the table, she held it reverently in her hands for a few minutes. When her tea was ready, she carried the Bible to the table with her and opened it randomly. It fell open to Matthew. The Sermon on the Mount. Her gaze landed on Matthew 5:4.

"Blessed are those who mourn—they will be comforted."

At that moment, she felt God's presence stronger than she had in the past three years. She had mourned. And if she let Him, her God would comfort her. She remained at the table for another hour, her tea forgotten as she deliberately set about spending time with the Lord and allowing Him to minister to her broken heart.

Irene was ready and waiting by the time Paul picked her up at eight. The boys had eaten breakfast and gone to school with Sergeant Zee. Irene couldn't quite bring herself to call the woman "Claire," even though she'd been invited to. For some reason, she felt safer sending her boys off with efficient Sergeant Zee than with the friendly, vivacious Claire. Strange, but that's the way a mother's heart worked sometimes.

Mary Ann was finishing up her breakfast, too. Rather, she was throwing her breakfast. Irene was busy cleaning the cereal up off the floor when the doorbell rang. Her pulse skittered.

"Okay, baby girl, we gotta get you all cleaned up and pretty. Hopefully, we'll find your parents today." She was careful not to say *mam* or *dat* so she wouldn't get the toddler worked up.

"Pow, Pow." Mary Ann shrieked happily.

Pow? Irene wrinkled her brow and searched through her vocabulary. Then it hit her. Mary Ann was trying to say "Paul," but the baby couldn't manage the *l* sound yet. Irene racked her brain for other words she'd heard Mary Ann say. There were only a handful, which wasn't odd. Maybe she had said words that were unclear and in Pennsylvania Dutch. Or maybe she had a language delay due to the Down syndrome. Either way, Irene didn't know how well her parents would take that one of her first words was the name of an Englisch cop. Well, they probably wouldn't care, she decided. They'd be so overjoyed at getting their baby back it wouldn't matter what she said.

Irene and Mary Ann went out to meet Paul. His eyes were covered with dark sunglasses today. She missed seeing his eyes, but had to admit he was gorgeous. Flushing, she put the baby in the car seat, wishing she hadn't braided her hair so it could provide some shielding to her red cheeks. She felt like a schoolgirl.

"Morning, Red." There was that smooth-as-velvet drawl.

It was going to be a long day.

"Good morning, Paul."

In the end, it wasn't as long a day as they'd expected. Mary Ann traveled very well, and kept up a long string of giggles and babbling from the back seat. Several times, Paul and Irene exchanged grins at the noises.

The trip was around five hours long, due to stops to eat or to get out and let Mary Ann stretch her legs or have her diaper changed. At one stop, Irene offered Paul a tin of homemade cookies, courtesy of her mom. As he took one, their fingers touched. Electricity shot up her arm. This time, she didn't pull away. This time, she stayed where she was and watched him as he watched her, unable to look away.

He's going to kiss me, she thought. *Maybe? Yes.* His head moved closer.

"Irene?"

Was he asking for permission? She didn't know what to do. It didn't matter. He seemed to take her lack of response as consent. His head came closer. She felt his breath on her lips.

"Pow! Pow!" Mary Ann toddled over and pushed herself in between them, jabbering away.

They'd almost kissed! She was in mortal danger, they were on a mission, and they'd almost kissed! What were they thinking?

She couldn't regret it, though. Her blood was still hammering in her veins.

"Well," she said, to relieve the tension, "at least we know she's not afraid of you anymore."

"Pow?" Paul frowned quizzically.

"That's how she says 'Paul,'" Irene relied gently.

His eyes widened. Then he did something that melted her heart. He leaned over and kissed the bonneted head. When he looked back at her, his eyes were shining.

That's how he'd look when his child said "Daddy" for the first time.

She shouldn't go there. Maybe when the case was behind them. But, for now, she needed to remember that there was a man out there whose mission it was to end her life. It was only a matter of time before he attacked again.

FOURTEEN

They arrived in Holmes County, Ohio, after one o'clock in the afternoon. Irene was amazed. She had thought there was a large Amish population where she lived. Here, though, the Amish community was bristling with activity. Buggies were everywhere.

It didn't take long to find the first address on Paul's list. It was quite a distance from most of the houses, but Irene wasn't surprised by that. According to Brenda, one of the criteria for the children they kidnapped was that the family lived out of the way. This place definitely qualified.

The woman who came to the door watched them warily. She wasn't exactly unhelpful, but neither was she able to give them any new information. Yes, their family had suffered an accident lately. Some of the local kids had been smoking in the barn. No one had died. They'd lost some farm equipment. She didn't recognize

Mary Ann, nor was she aware of any missing children with Down syndrome.

Irene sighed, discouraged, as they started driving again.

"Hey, now, don't do that." Paul reached out and put his hand on her shoulder, squeezing gently. "We now have one less place on our list. Which means the probability of one the next houses being the right one has gone up proportionally."

Irene laughed, shaking her head. "You've been spending too much time with Miles. That's the sort of geeky thing he would say."

Paul laughed with her. There was no rancor in the words or the laughter. The sergeant was dear to them all.

The next house was much the same as the first, although this time there were several children about and a couple of youths working in the barn. They were very kind. Irene liked them immensely.

But they were not Mary Ann's family.

"I will pray that Gott will lead you to the right family," the woman said.

"Thank you. We appreciate it," Irene returned. Paul raised an eyebrow. She smiled back. She had meant every word.

They returned to the car and resumed driving. By now, Mary Ann had grown tired of traveling. She cried and tried to wiggle out of her seat. When she couldn't get free, she shrieked. Irene was afraid she'd have a headache before they arrived at the next place.

But arrive they did.

"Are we interrupting some kind of event, do you think?"

There were buggies and people everywhere. Kids and adults. Despite the cold weather, there was a crowd of people outside. On one side of the house was a large hill. She could see children sledding on it.

"I don't know. I guess we'll find out." Paul said.

Sighing, she nodded and got out of the car. Their arrival had a domino effect. People stopped what they were doing to watch the unknown Englischers get out of the police cruiser. Irene immediately went to the back to retrieve Mary Ann. The child's shrieks filled the air as Irene opened the door.

If they didn't have someone's attention before, they had it now.

Thankfully, the crying stopped abruptly when Irene unstrapped her from the car seat. As soon as Irene reappeared with a suddenly smiling Mary Ann in her arms a murmur spread through the crowd. Irene saw one of the children run into the house.

"Mam!" the child yelled.

Within seconds, the door flew open, and adults spilled from the house. In the front was a pretty Amish woman with a black dress and red hair peeping out from under her bonnet. Her pale cheeks were wet, tears flooding down them. Right behind her came a man, crying, as well.

Mary Ann saw them and reacted as if she'd been electrified. She shrieked and shook and struggled in Irene's arms. Irene set her down. "Mam. Da. Mam. Da." The words tumbled out of her little mouth, over and over.

Her parents rushed to their baby and knelt to embrace her, paying no attention to the snow. Their reaction, the love and joy on the faces, was so similar to that of Edith's parents.

"We knew our baby was not dead," Mary Ann's father stated, rising to greet the newcomers. "How did you find her?"

Irene let Paul take the lead on this one. She was overcome watching the touching reunion.

"She was kidnapped by people who wanted to sell her in an adoption scam."

Both parents gaped at Paul, apparently dumbfounded.

"How did you rescue her?" Mrs. Lapp whispered, her face distraught.

Irene finally spoke up. "One of the kidnappers had a change of heart. She hid Mary Ann in my car when I left it unlocked."

She decided not to go into the rest—such as Eddie's plans for disposing of Mary Ann.

Paul rubbed her shoulder. Reassurance?

All too soon it was time to go. She suddenly realized how much she was going to miss Mary Ann.

"Can I give her a hug? To say goodbye?"

Mary Ann's mother nodded and stepped back slightly so Irene could move in closer. Irene squatted near the little girl. "Hey, Mary Ann, I need a hug. Paul and I are going bye-bye."

Mary Ann put up her tiny arms, and Irene wrapped her in one last hug. As much as she'd miss her, she was at total peace. This was exactly where the precious child belonged.

Irene set her down and looked into her sweet face. "You be good, darling girl."

When Irene stood, Mary Ann seemed to search for something. Then her arms raised again. "Pow. Pow."

As long as she lived, she knew she'd never forget the sudden sweetness on his face. Or the way his deep eyes glistened. He copied the posture Irene had used to embrace the child and pulled her into his arms. "Bye, Mary Ann." Then he moved so they were nose to nose. He whispered, but his words were still audible. "I promised we'd find your *mam* and *dat*. Be happy, sweetheart."

"Pow." She patted his face.

They returned to the car and started driving back home. The drive was silent. Irene was too wrung out to speak. And worried. Now that they had found Mary Ann's parents, they only had one more task. And that was to find Billy—before he found her.

Pensive, she sighed. Paul reached out and covered her hand with his. He didn't say anything, but she was grateful for the comfort. If only she could make her nerves settle down.

Billy Sharps was out there somewhere. And she knew he wasn't going to give up.

They still had to find the man targeting Irene. Paul felt as if the stakes had just been raised. Billy had no remaining coconspirators, the money he'd left at the house had been taken as evidence and the children he'd stolen had been returned. His officers had interviewed Eddie. He'd agreed to cooperate in return for a lighter sentence and give the authorities all the information on the families who'd bought the children.

That left Billy to focus his vengeance on Irene. Paul could see her out of his periphery.

Tension held her body stiff, her face grim. He had a pretty good idea that Billy was on her mind, too.

They were pulling into a town. He could see a restaurant on the left side. His stomach had grumbled for the past half hour, and he'd seen her rub hers. Making a split-second decision, he pulled into a spot on the street, as close to the streetlight as he could get.

"Come on. We need to stretch our legs. Might as well eat."

It was an Amish-run restaurant. He grinned in anticipation. No one cooked like Amish women. This would be a treat, even if they still needed to be careful.

Paul requested one of the tables near the window. He made sure that he sat where he could see the car the entire meal. He didn't want another bomb planted. Or any kind of tracking device. Now that he knew the perp was ex-military, that opened the door to all kinds of modes of attack. He needed to be on his guard.

The food was all homemade, delicious and there was lots of it. They declined dessert, and got up. As they walked to the door, Paul reached out and took hold of Irene's hand. He had no idea how she'd respond. Pull away? Let her hand stay in his?

She sent him a saucy smile and a tilted eyebrow. That was fine. It was progress.

Outside the restaurant, though, he dropped her hand as they approached the car. He kept her close to the building so he could shield her.

It seemed like forever before they reached the cruiser. Soon he'd be able to relax. Not yet.

A shadow moved.

"Down!"

Paul shoved Irene to the ground and threw himself on top of her. Not a second too soon. The closest vehicle next to theirs—a buggy— exploded, sending waves of heat over them. The wheels flew through the air.

People started screaming. The restaurant patrons streamed out the door in an angry mass. When no further blasts seemed to be coming, Paul sat up carefully. Irene remained where she lay on the ground, coughing weakly. At a quick once-over, she appeared uninjured.

"Irene! Are you okay?" He seemed to be asking that question a lot lately.

"Yeah." She sat up, dazed, and stared stunned at the burning buggy. "Was anyone in that thing? Where is the horse?"

"I put my horse in the barn out back," a shaky voice replied.

They looked up to see a middle-aged man, watching his mode of transportation burn before his eyes. Paul stood and faced the crowd, making sure to keep himself between them and Irene. Her back was to the building, so there was little chance that anyone would be able to sneak in behind her.

Irene wilted, leaning back against the bricks. He felt the same way. The destruction was senseless and cruel, but at least everyone had survived—it would have been horrible if any person or horse had been killed in the blast.

"Did anyone see anything? Anyone acting suspicious near the buggy in the past hour, or anyone running after it blew?"

"Ja," a soft voice replied. "I saw someone." A young woman wearing a pale dress stepped forward, shivering. Cold? Or fear? She was wearing a coat and gloves, making it likely that she had already been outside before the blast. No one seemed to have grabbed a coat when they left the restaurant.

Paul motioned the girl forward. He wasn't moving from Irene. If there was a sniper out there, they'd have to go through him first. No one touched his woman. He was tired of trying to pretend he didn't love her. Well, he did, whether or not she felt the same way. He would stand by her and protect her while she remained in danger. Or longer, if she allowed him to remain in her life.

The girl had come to stand before him. She tried to remain still, although he could discern telltale signs of nervousness—twisting her hands, chewing her lip, her eyes darting around.

"It's okay, miss. You're not in any trouble. But the man responsible for this is a dangerous criminal and we need to catch him as soon as possible. He has been kidnapping Amish children and selling them. My companion and I have just come from returning one of those children to her family."

An angry murmur spread through the crowd. Children were to be protected. The idea of stealing a child was repugnant.

"I didn't see him put anything in the buggy. But right before it happened, I saw a man standing over there—" She pointed to an area off to the left. He would have been blocked from Paul's view by the buggy. "As you came out, he pointed something at the buggy. I thought it was a cell phone. He touched it with his other hand, and then the buggy exploded."

"How is it that you weren't hurt by it?" Paul was struck with how close the teenager had come to being seriously injured.

"I was standing on the other side of that truck. I could see everything through its window."

"Did you see him leave?" Paul really hoped she had.

"*Nee*. I mean no. I looked up and he was gone." She looked worried.

"It's okay," he reassured her. "Can you tell me anything about what he looked like?"

Even before she described him, Paul knew what she'd say. She'd seen a dark-haired man in a camouflage coat. William Sharps.

Paul and Irene were both exhausted by the time they reached Mrs. Tucker's house that evening. Paul walked her inside.

"Chief Paul! Mommy!" Matthew skidded to a halt before them and threw his arms around first his mother and then the chief. Paul started to do his customary rubbing of the boy's head, but stopped, affection stealing over him. Instead, he bent down and returned Matthew's hug. Matthew grinned.

Paul started to straighten, then noticed AJ standing at his side, his face serious. AJ was harder to read. Did he want a hug? Paul didn't know what to do. He decided to leave it up to the seven-year-old and opened his arms. Immediately, AJ's thin face lit up and he bounded in to accept a hug, gripping Paul tightly in return.

Paul had made up his mind earlier to go straight home and leave Irene to have some personal time with her sons. So when Vera invited him to stay and have a piece of pecan pie and a cup of fresh coffee, he opened his mouth to decline.

Irene's soft hand on his arm stopped him.

"Paul, we'd love to have you join us." She added a soft smile meant only for him. He forgot how to breathe. "Stay."

Wordlessly, he nodded.

Pecan pie was his absolute favorite. And yet this time, he never tasted a bite. His focus was all on the beautiful redhead seated next to him. He would gladly remain by her side for the rest of his days. As far as he was concerned, there'd never be another woman for him.

It was some time later when he looked around to see Vera herding the boys off to their baths. They both came over to give Paul and their mother another hug before following their grandmother.

Paul stood up. He needed to take his leave.

As they moved together to the front door, his phone rang. It was Jackson.

"Jackson. What's going on?" He kept his eyes on Irene as he talked.

"Hey, Chief. We just got a report that Sharps might have been spotted near the Indiana border."

That grabbed his attention. His brow wrinkled as he processed this new information. "Indiana? Not Pennsylvania?"

"That's what the report said. It wasn't a definite sighting, but the timing's right."

He hung up and related the news to Irene. "I'm still going to have you watched and the house kept under surveillance. Even if it's him leaving the area for now, I don't think he'll stay gone. The Indiana police are keeping a watch for him, also."

"You'll get him." Irene flashed that soft smile up at him. The one that made him feel invincible and weak at the knees simultaneously. "I know you will, Paul. I have faith in you."

He couldn't take any more. He reached out and pulled her gently into his arms, the way he'd wanted to so many times. He held his breath, waiting for her to resist or pull back. She did neither, melting into his arms. Softly, he allowed his lips to touch hers. A sigh left her. Gaining confidence, he kissed her again, letting the sweet kiss linger.

When they parted, her cheeks were pink and her eyes were shining.

Touching the side of her face, he turned and walked out the door, knowing he'd dream of this moment all night.

FIFTEEN

Irene waved at the officer sitting across the street in his cruiser the next afternoon as she left her office and headed toward her car to drive to a meeting. Paul had reluctantly agreed to let her go to work, as long as an officer trailed her. The Erie precinct had sent several officers to help provide coverage. One of them was Lieutenant Crane. He didn't wave back. She shrugged. He wasn't there to be social. She squinted, trying to see him better.

Nope. The glare from the sun was too sharp. She could see his position but not his face. She slowed her walk. A sudden chill fell over her. She continued rapidly on stiff legs to where her SUV was parked. She could almost feel icy fingers touching her neck and couldn't keep her shoulders from twitching.

Her thoughts flew back to the officer who was on duty to protect her. Even if he wasn't feeling friendly, he should have acknowledged her presence. Maybe he hadn't seen her wave? She cut her eyes to the cruiser. He was sitting in the same position as before.

Something was not right.

She reached her vehicle and began to get in, then hesitated. Miles's fiancée, Rebecca, had been attacked by someone hiding in her car back in October, she remembered. Her legs shook as she peered in her windows. Some of the tension fled as she ascertained that no one was in her car.

But that didn't mean there was no danger.

She dove into the vehicle, hitting the lock button as soon as the door slammed behind her. Then she leaned her head back against the headrest and let out a shuddering breath. But she couldn't rest easy yet. Turning her car on, she jabbed the phone button on the dashboard. Her phone was in her back pocket, but it was close enough for the Bluetooth signal to pick up.

"Number?" the computerized voice queried.

Breathlessly, she gave Paul's number, rooting around in her purse for her sunglasses. Her instinct told her to get out of there, but with the way the sun was reflecting off the snow, she knew she'd never be able to drive without shades. Blue eyes were just that sensitive.

A moment later she sighed in resignation.

Voice mail. Well, she'd leave the message as she drove away. Setting her sunglasses on the bridge of her nose, she clutched the gearshift to put the car in Reverse.

And shrieked as something hit her window. Her shriek melded with the beep from the voice mail.

Turning her head, she saw a gun pointing right at her.

Private William Sharps had found her. She could still take her chances and put the car in Reverse, hoping to get away before he shot her. Then she saw what he had in his other hand, and her heart stopped beating.

Matthew's stuffed crocodile. He'd never lose sight of it.

Terrified that this man had her kids, she rolled the window down.

"Smart lady," he sneered. "Get out of the car and come with me if you want your brats to live."

"What do want from me?" She hated the quaver in her voice, but she was still composed enough to realize that whatever was said was being recorded in Paul's voice mail. It was her only hope of getting out of this alive. She knew without a doubt that the man in front of her planned to kill her. And probably her children, too.

Lord, help us. Please guide me.

The sneer hardened into a look of pure hatred. "It's all your fault. If not for you, Niko would still be alive, and we'd be on our way to being rich men."

"You know the police are after you." His eyes blazed at her words, and she hoped the anger provoked him into saying something—revealing an important clue. She had to give Paul as much as information as she could. "Your friend Eddie is in jail. You don't want to add another murder to your list of offenses."

He let out a crack of harsh laughter. It grated along her sensitive nerves. "Yeah, Eddie's probably told them everything. What a weak fool! He wanted to go into hiding again. Said we'd start again in another state. Plenty of desperate people all over the country willing to pay for children. You were too close with the police, he said. It was too risky to continue to work the operation in Pennsylvania. But what about what I wanted?"

She didn't answer. The malevolent stare he leveled at her said he didn't care what she thought. He'd made up his mind.

He kicked the door. She jumped, her pulse leaping. "Get out. You're going to do exactly what I say if you want your kids to survive.

They'll be orphans, but they may live. *If* you follow my directions."

At that, she knew it was doubtful that she would be rescued in time. But she wasn't giving up. Not while there was a chance that her babies would survive.

She must have hesitated too long. He kicked the door again and pointed the gun straight at her head.

"I have no problem with shooting you right here in the middle of the street. But if I do, your kids won't survive the day."

Numbly, she opened the door and stepped down. She didn't even take the time to turn off the engine. Who knew what would set him off? She suspected he wouldn't really shoot her out in the open. Judging by the angle at which he was standing, he was trying to hide the gun from any passersby. Plus, there was no silencer on it, so chances were he'd be seen if he shot her and ran. No, he was bluffing, though she couldn't exactly call his bluff. Not if her goal was to get both herself and AJ and Matthew out of this horrific nightmare alive.

No sooner had she stepped away from her vehicle than her right elbow was yanked into his side. Her skin crawled at being in such close proximity to a killer. His long legs kept up a brisk pace and she was forced to jog along at his side, the click of her boot heels loud in the silence. Once, she tripped.

His grip tightened, and he pulled her arm behind her at a painful angle.

Near the side of the parking lot, he stopped next to an old pickup truck. It was so rusted she could barely tell what the original color had been. He forced her up into the cab, shoving her over so he could climb up beside her. He gave her one final shove. Hard. Just for spite, she was sure of it. Her knee knocked over a can of Diet Coke. It spilled across the passenger seat. Her head cracked against the window. She bit her lip to keep from crying out and tasted blood.

Sharps slammed his door shut, then reached behind his seat and pulled out a roll of duct tape. Instinctively, she drew back. He slapped her, then grabbed both wrists in one large hand. The tape made a loud, tearing noise as he wound it around and around her wrists tight enough that she worried about losing circulation. When he was satisfied that she couldn't escape, he started the engine and began to drive.

Sharps drove one-handed, the other hand holding the gun. It was positioned low enough that bystanders couldn't see it. But Irene never forgot that it was there. Add to that, he had no heat in the truck, and her seat was wet. Soon, she was shivering from a combination of terror and the cold seeping into her body. Her mind was unable to formulate clear thoughts. She should pray, but nothing was coming. Instead, her mind kept up a litany of *Help, Lord. Help.*

It was all she could do. She trusted that God understood, and that He would take care of the rest.

Finally, Sharps pulled off the main road and up a side street. She knew this road. It dead-ended at an old lumber mill that had been closed for over ten years.

Apparently, Sharps had found another use for it.

Shudders were racking her slender frame continuously by this point. Her jaw was aching from her chattering teeth grinding against each other.

Sharps stopped the truck next to the boarded-up building and got out. He dragged her across the seat without any thought to her bound hands. When she fell out of the truck and landed in a heap at his feet, he kicked her, then yanked her upright.

"Okay, woman," he growled. "It's time you got what was coming to you."

He pushed her forward. She cried out as her heel caught in a crack and her ankle twisted. He didn't care, just kept herding her toward the building. Inside, the only positive thing she could determine was that the building was slightly warmer than outside. She was so frozen, though, she wasn't sure she'd ever truly be warm again.

Not that she had all that long to feel cold.

Her frantic gaze searched the shadows for any sign of her babies. But neither AJ nor Matthew was anywhere to be seen.

Was she too late?

"Where are my sons?" she demanded, fear forgotten in her concern for her children.

He laughed, a horrible sound. "I ain't got your kids. Never did. Followed them this morning and the little one dropped the animal. Knew I could use it as bait. You weren't so smart, were ya? Now I have you here, and no one knows any better."

He didn't have her boys. That meant she could fight back without them being in danger.

Lord, help me. And please let Paul find me. I love him, Lord. And I think he loves me.

Her hands were still bound. As Sharps advanced on her, she backed away, looking around for anything she might use to defend herself. As she passed a rickety shelf unit, she noticed a pile of old straw and insulation that was being used for a mouse's nest. Her wrists were bound, but she could still use her hands. Before she could talk herself out of it, she grabbed it up in her fists and threw it directly at his eyes. A mouse fell out of the debris and landed on him, biting his cheek in its fright.

Sharps shrieked, waving his arms to rid himself of both the rodent and the debris in his eyes.

Irene didn't stick around to watch. Whirling, she took off as fast as her boots would let her run.

Not fast enough. Within seconds, she heard him charging after her.

There was a room ahead of her. She ran in and shoved the door shut, locking it with the slide latch.

He banged on the door. Each bang brought a shower of dust. The door frame shook. It wouldn't last long under the onslaught.

And then he would catch her.

Paul glanced at the clock on the wall. Three fifteen. Irene would be at work for another hour. He knew she had a meeting this afternoon. Officer Crane was watching her. Paul frowned as he realized that Crane should have reported in already.

A knock on the door startled him. His head shot up. His two new hires were waiting for him. He waved them in. Officer Lily Shepherd entered, followed by Officer Gabe McLachlan.

Both had neutral expressions, but he could read the apprehension in their eyes. He smothered a grin. Facing the new chief was always a harrowing experience. Part of him was tempted to growl at them just to see their reactions. Of course, he wouldn't. He'd been the new guy before. And he'd also been the one shown mercy, so he would do likewise.

"Relax, you two. I just wanted to review a few details before you go on duty for the first time here."

Shepherd's shoulders dipped just a little, some of the tightness flowing out. McLachlan grinned and shook his head. Paul smiled back. He couldn't help it. His gut feeling was that they would both be assets to his team.

"Sit down. I want to see how you're settling in."

They had both attended an orientation. He knew neither officer was from the area. Shepherd had started out in Chicago. Her record working the streets there was impressive. Mac was from the other side of Pittsburgh.

They each grabbed a chair in front of the desk and sat, waiting for him to begin.

Paul lowered himself into his chair and reached for the files on the desk. His eyes went to the clock again. Almost three twenty. His gut screamed that something was wrong—it wasn't like Crane to be late checking in. He'd known the Erie officer for years. He hadn't become chief by ignoring his instincts. He considered them a gift from God to help him perform his duties.

"Hold on a minute, guys." He grabbed his phone. "I need to check in with Crane for a moment."

He didn't wait for them to agree.

The light on his phone was blinking. He pushed the button and tapped in his access code to unlock it. He smiled, relief leaking through his system. A voice mail. Well, Crane must have called in and he hadn't heard the phone ring. That was fine.

He tapped the voice-mail icon and held the phone up to his ear to listen in.

The smile slid off his face. He heard Irene gasp. Why didn't she say something? Then fear plowed into his brain. Someone was talking. The voice was unfamiliar, but the menace was clear.

"Smart lady. Get out of the car and come with me if you want your brats to live."

Sharps had Irene! And possibly her kids!

It took all his will to force himself to stand and listen to the rest of the message, hoping against hope the killer would reveal a location or some other pertinent detail. Nothing.

He had no time to waste. The moment the call was done, he was around his desk and heading to the door.

"You two, with me," he barked to the startled officers. Both Shepherd and Mac rose immediately and followed without question. "Jackson!"

Gavin Jackson looked up from his desk.

"Let all precincts know. Billy Sharps has Irene. Parker." He pointed a finger at the brown-haired sergeant. His finger shook, but he ignored it, as well as the agony pulsing through his system. If Irene died, he wasn't sure how he'd cope with that. "You need to check in with Zee at Mrs. Tucker's house. If they are there and safe, let me know. Tell Zee no one leaves. They may be in danger."

Parker nodded and reached for his phone.

"Thompson!" he barked. "Go back to the hospital and see if the woman in custody, Brenda, knows of another possible place Sharps might take someone. Anything she can think of may help. Move, people! Lives are in danger!"

The officers scattered, their faces grim. Irene Martello was well liked by all of them. And even if she had been a stranger, Paul knew he could count on every single one of them to put their lives on the line to protect her. It was their calling. And they were all dedicated to it.

"You two—" He waved a finger between McLachlan and Shepherd. "I want you with me."

They didn't question him. They may have been newly hired, but both had strong service records.

He didn't bother weighing the pros and cons of siren or no siren. He was going in hot. Irene needed him. He would die before he let her down. Cars parted, moving to the side of the road to allow his cruiser with its blazing red-and-blue lights to pass.

Paul's phone rang. Parker's name flashed up on the display. Paul jabbed the phone button, putting him on speaker.

"Yeah, Parker. What do you have?"

"Chief, I talked with Zee. Mrs. Tucker and the kids are safe. The doors are bolted."

"Good. Keep me informed of any developments."

"You got it." A pause. "Chief? We'll be praying for Irene. And for you."

Paul had to swallow around the lump that had gathered in his throat. "Thanks, Ryan. It means a lot."

He caught McLachlan's puzzled glance in the mirror. Well, now was not the time or place to spill his heart. Lord willing, he'd be able to find Irene. Alive. And if he did, he'd never let his past cause him to keep his heart from her again. Right now, however, he needed to focus. Praying silently, he drove to where Irene worked. Her car was still there in the parking lot. His mouth went dry. The driver's door was wide-open, and the motor was still running. Irene was nowhere to be seen.

He pulled behind Crane's cruiser. "McLachlan. Shepherd. Go search that SUV. Make note of any signs of struggle. Anything we can use."

Meanwhile, he opened his own door and stood, letting his training and experience kick in. Scanning the area, he judged that the danger here was gone, then went to check on Crane. He had a bad feeling about it. Crane was an older officer with decades of experience. He wouldn't have let Irene go with a stranger. Even if he'd been distracted or away from his car, the sight of her door being open would have clued him in that something was wrong.

So it was no surprise to find that the cheerful grandfather of two had been shot. Twice. There was a gash along the side of his head. And the other bullet was in his chest. His Kevlar vest had stopped it from killing him. Even as he watched, Paul could see his friend's chest rising and falling. The passenger window was shattered, glass strewn all over the seat. Paul opened the passenger door. He could hear Crane breathe. And groan. It sounded beautiful.

"Hold on, buddy. I'm calling for help." Paul immediately thumbed the radio on his shoulder and called in for an ambulance.

He heard feet running behind him.

"Sir!" Shepherd halted, her eyes excited. "Mac found something, sir!"

And indeed, Mac had found something.

"See these tracks, sir?" Mac pointed at a fresh set of tire tracks, not yet covered by snow. "They're recent, because it snowed up until almost three. And there are footprints."

Paul squatted. "Yep. See these? Heels. Like those fancy boots Irene wears."

"Exactly. And they both stop near the same side of the tracks. It looks like he must have had her get into his vehicle, then he got in the same side. But she was walking, so she was alive. And, I found this."

He handed Paul a small piece of paper. Paul almost crowed with delight. It was a gas receipt from a nearby gas station. From less than two hours ago.

"Outstanding work, you two," he praised them, feeling the first ray of hope. "If we can get a description of the vehicle, we'll be able to put out an alert."

Trying not to let his excitement get away

with him, Paul ordered Mac to remain on the scene until the paramedics came. "I'm going to have Parker meet you at the hospital. I want you to search with him as soon as we have more information. Shepherd," he said as he turned to the woman beside him. "You're with me. I hope we won't need to call on your experience, but I want someone with sniper training, just in case."

Her eyes were shadowed, but she nodded in agreement.

They were off. Fortunately, the clerk at the gas station did remember the truck. Although there had been a lot of traffic at the time in question, most of the customers had been women in smaller vehicles or SUV drivers out Christmas shopping. The only man to fit Sharps's description had made himself even more memorable by acting suspiciously while at the pumps. So much so that she had secretly written down the make and model of the full-size pickup truck he was driving and the license plate. When he came in, he'd been rude, but hadn't done anything else, so she had set the number aside.

Paul thanked her and immediately put out an alert for the vehicle and driver. If all went well, they'd be able to track him down fast.

Paul just prayed it was in time.

SIXTEEN

Paul's phone rang. He snatched it out of his pocket. It was McLachlan.

"Mac, what do ya got?"

"Chief, Parker and I are just leaving the hospital. The girlfriend remembered our guy talking to his cousin about an old lumberyard they could use as a secret base if things ever went south. She was pretty sure it was within an hour of here."

Paul thought for a moment. "I know of a couple. One near Cochranton. Another close to Meadville."

He called the others, having them divide up, searching all possibilities.

He headed for Meadville, hating the fact that it might be a wild-goose chase. But until he had more facts, it was all he could do.

His phone buzzed again. It was Jackson. He jabbed the phone button with more force than necessary. Shepherd shot him a wide-eyed glance, then her expression went flat again.

"Chief!" Jackson's voice was sharper than usual, highlighting the strain they were all feeling. "The Cochranton police said that truck was spotted in Cochranton earlier this morning. It was crossing the bridge. Heading away from where the old lumber mill is."

"On my way."

Paul flipped on his siren, then did a U-turn at the next intersection. Shepherd used the radio to advise the others of the new information. Paul swerved onto the route that would take them to Cochranton. It was a relief that the road crews had recently been through there. The roads were relatively clear, letting him go at a normal speed. Unfortunately, he couldn't go any faster than that. There were so many twists and turns in these Pennsylvania roads. One turn taken too fast and they'd be stuck in a ditch. Which would mean he wouldn't be able to get to Irene.

It took less than thirty minutes, but it was the longest drive he'd ever experienced. The woman he loved, and if he was honest with himself, had loved since high school, was in danger. *Please, Lord. Keep her safe.*

As they approached the old mill, he turned off his sirens. No use letting the madman holding Irene know that he'd been located. Pulling off before the mill, he and Shepherd exited the cruiser and walked into the yard.

The truck was there.

Paul could have cried, his relief was so great.

But it was too early to celebrate. Irene was still inside with Sharps. Mac and Parker jogged quietly into sight. He heard Shepherd quietly talking into her radio, letting the other teams know their status. Jackson's voice replied he was en route. Approximate arrival in five minutes. Good. His team was coming in. There would be no escape for this villain.

Scooting close to the building, he motioned for the others to spread out, covering all the exits. When they complied, he moved. Gently he opened the door a mere inch, listening for any clues as to the location of Sharps and Irene.

Deep inside the structure, a man was yelling. Although he couldn't make out all the words, he could understand enough. Vile, angry threats of torture and death.

He'd never been so happy to hear such awful language in his life. It meant Irene was still alive. And fighting. Because she was evidently hiding.

Banging. Loud banging. A fist on wood.

A shot.

The acid in his stomach churned. What had been shot?

More yelling. Enraged.

It was time to get in there. Indicating to Shepherd that he needed her to come with him, he entered the lumber mill. The smell of dust, mold and rotting wood was overpowering. There was also the tangy smell that told him rodents had taken up residence.

"See if you can sneak up behind him. If need be, I will distract him, giving you a chance to shoot," he whispered. Shepherd's face was troubled. He reinforced his priority. "Irene is the most important thing here. Her safety, and the safety of my officers, has to be my focus."

Understanding dawned. Yes, he would sacrifice himself for Irene to live. There was never any doubt that he'd do that. Willingly. She nodded.

He followed the sounds and his heart froze as a woman cried out.

Irene.

Paul broke into a run. Sharps had Irene by the hair and was dragging her out from behind an old filing cabinet. His gun was in his other hand. He yanked Irene to him and started to lift the gun.

Paul had to act, now.

"Sharps!" he shouted, breaking the man's focus. "Police! Let her go!"

Former Private William Sharps whirled, still holding Irene. "Back off! I'll kill her!" he screamed. Paul knew he was serious. There was no sign of Shepherd yet. She may not have been able to find a way around. It was a chilling possibility. He needed to give her more time. There was no way he could shoot Sharps right now without hitting Irene.

"Killing her won't bring your cousin back. It was never our intention that he die. No one else needs to die here."

Sharps sneered. "Like you're just gonna let me go? Don't come any closer!"

Paul stopped. He had been inching forward.

"I ain't afraid to use this gun! I already killed one cop today, so I know there's no way out for me."

Irene paled. Paul could see the shudder that went through her. She had probably wondered about Crane.

"He's not dead!" Paul said, using his most reasonable voice, which was a challenge, because he was shouting inside. "You didn't kill a cop, you just injured him. He's on his way to the hospital now."

He hoped.

The young man scowled, but then his grip on

the gun tightened. And his grip on Irene. "No. I don't believe you. You'd say anything to get me to let her go."

He placed the gun against Irene's temple. Her eyes closed, lips moving. She was praying. Sweat beaded on his forehead.

A door's squeaky hinges creaked behind them. Sharps whirled, pointing the gun in that direction even as he hauled Irene closer, his arm around her throat. Paul shot the gun out of his hand at the same moment that Irene slammed the heel of her boot against his shin. He howled, releasing her.

"Irene! Run!" Paul ordered, his voice hoarse.

She took off toward the door. Parker was there, waiting for her. He grabbed her and pulled her outside.

"Don't worry about me!" she yelled. "Go help Paul!"

There was nothing he could do about the tiny burst of pleasure that shot through him at the evidence that she was concerned for him. He focused on the man in front of him. Sharps was clutching his hand to his stomach, blood dripping on the sawdust-covered floor.

Paul eased closer, gun still pointed at him. "It's over, Billy. Put your hands up."

Sharps let out a whimper and began to raise his hands. Paul stepped closer. He was less than two feet away. The killer started gagging, his throat working as he made retching sounds and started to bend over. In the next moment, he hurtled himself at Paul, a blade glinting in his hands.

Paul felt the sudden stabbing pain, then heard a shot from behind. Sharps slipped off Paul and onto the ground, screaming.

Shepherd had hit her target.

Too bad she was too late.

Paul felt himself topple over and was out before he hit the ground.

What was going on in there?

Irene paced, worrying her lower lip between her teeth. Paul had told her to run, so she had. She knew that the worst thing she could have done at a time like this would have been to stay and distract him and the other cops. Staying would have inhibited their ability to respond to the threat Sharps represented.

She knew that in her head, but in her heart, she felt she had abandoned Paul. The man who had stepped up to be her protector. The man who—and now she could admit it—she'd fallen in love with.

Something was wrong. She'd heard a shot, and there'd been screaming. Then another shot.

Now the police officers around her were all converging on the building.

One phrase penetrated her mind. *The chief's been injured.*

A dark chasm opened inside her. Paul had been hurt. She had no idea how bad. Was he even still alive? She tried to get to the building, but the officer at the door wouldn't let her through.

"Sorry, Mrs. Martello," the young woman said quietly. "This is a crime scene. And I can't let you contaminate it."

Irene stared at her. Even in her grief, she recognized a kindred soul. This woman had seen love and loss before. She understood. "Is he… I mean is Paul—"

She couldn't say the words. They were too raw, would make it too real.

"No. He's not dead. He's been stabbed, and is losing a lot of blood. That's all I can tell you."

She hated it, but Irene had to be satisfied with that until the ambulance arrived. When it pulled up, Seth got out with Sydney. He squeezed her shoulder as they walked past. They seemed to be inside forever. When they exited, carrying Paul on a stretcher, she gasped. A dark stain had spread out across his shirt. His shoulder was covered with several layers of thick bandages. It must have been bleeding heavily. She knew her first aid. You apply bandages and pressure until the bleeding stopped. The ragged sound of his breathing was loud. Everyone was silent as he passed. His ashen complexion terrified her.

Tears ran down her face, but she ignored them. Her heart was breaking.

Not again. She thought she'd die from the pain of losing Tony. She couldn't bear to lose Paul, too. Oh, why had she opened herself up to this kind of grief again?

She wished Jace were back. She could really use her big brother right about now.

She began to step toward the stretcher and was stopped by a hand touching her arm. Jackson stood beside her. She was aware of Dan Willis taking position on her other side. Other officers moved in every direction. Everyone was pale, their eyes as somber as she had ever seen them. Paul was a man who commanded great respect and affection in those who worked with him.

"Irene."

She looked over at Dan.

"He needs to get to the hospital quickly," Dan said.

"I'm going with him." It wasn't a question. She wouldn't give way on this one. Not a chance. To her surprise, no one argued. Or maybe that was not surprising. They were very observant. No doubt, everyone knew that she was falling for the chief.

"I figured" was all Dan said. He helped her into the ambulance. She was aware dimly of the vehicle moving, its siren blaring, but her attention was focused on the dear man in front of her.

The ride to the hospital seemed to take forever. Irene held Paul's hand in hers, eyes glued to his pale face. He stirred once, opening those deep, dark eyes to see her.

"Irene," he murmured as his lids drifted shut again. "My Irene."

Her throat constricted. In her mind, she replayed her memories of Paul. Paul laughing in high school. Paul charming as he flirted with her. Paul cold and distant as he avoided her after he left her at the dance. Paul standing up next to Jace on his wedding day. Paul holding her face as he kissed her. Was that really only last night?

So many memories in her life were centered around this man. The thought of him suddenly disappearing from her life was devastating. But, if he lived, she would always have the worry hanging over her that this could happen again. What if he got hurt? What if he didn't come home? Maybe she'd been naive once, thinking such things didn't happen in LaMar Pond. But she had seen too much in the past few years to believe that anymore.

They arrived at the hospital, and she walked beside the stretcher as it was brought in through the emergency room entrance. Then she was left behind as the man she loved was wheeled into surgery. She called her mom, holding back tears as she talked to her babies. Her mom wanted to come, but Irene convinced her to stay home. This wasn't a place for kids.

For the next two hours, she paced aimlessly across the waiting room. The room began to fill with people. Paul's officers. Their wives. Dan came in and gave her a crushing hug. She held on for a moment, needing the connection. When she pulled back, her face was wet and his eyes were too bright. Parker and Jackson stood together, not talking though she had the impression they were giving each other support. The two new cops—she couldn't remember their names—also stood together. The woman wore a shuttered expression. Brooding. Her companion's face was openly concerned for Paul and—she guessed—for his fellow officer.

Melanie and Maggie sat with her, offering whatever comfort they could.

She felt apart from it all. Oh, none of them

had done anything to leave her out. In her numbness, she had a disconnected feeling. Would she ever be able to feel anything again?

"Irene."

And just like that, she shattered.

Jace was back. She hadn't heard him come up to her, but there he and Miles were. Weeping, she flung herself into his arms and buried her head in her brother's shoulder. Her tears turned into great heaving sobs. Jace wrapped his strong arms around her, rocking her as if she were a baby instead of a twenty-nine-year-old woman.

She had no clue how long she cried. When she finally lifted her head, she was almost dizzy from it.

"When did you get back?"

Jace brushed a hair back from her face, almost like a parent. She'd made the same motion with her children.

"Not long ago. We came straight here from the airport." Jace kissed her forehead.

Irene opened her mouth and forgot what she wanted to say. She had just noticed that all the officers had come and gathered around her and Jace. Not to gawk. There was something almost protective in their stance, and their expressions were full of compassion.

She felt stupid, letting herself lose control in front of Paul's colleagues.

Then she realized something. "Wait, Jace. Paul's mom and sister. Did anyone call them?"

Jackson responded. "I did. Mrs. Kennedy is on her way. Cammie is catching the first plane. They should both be here by this evening."

Good. She couldn't imagine not being able to be there if one of her children needed her.

Talking ceased when the doctor entered the waiting room. His face appeared solemn, but it was softened by the tiniest smile curling at the edges.

"I'm assuming that you folks are all here for Chief Kennedy?"

As one they nodded.

"How is he, Doctor?" Irene stepped forward. If any of the cops felt it odd that she was the one asking, none of them said anything. They seemed to accept it as her right. So how obvious had her feelings been, anyway?

"The surgery went well. Chief Kennedy was very fortunate. The knife missed the carotid artery. The muscle damage was minimal. He will need lots of rest, but should make a complete recovery."

The cheer that went up was so enthusiastic that Irene expected someone to run in and yell at them to quiet down. No one did, though.

Weakness invaded her knees. She stumbled over to a chair and sat, leaning her head back against the wall and closing her eyes. The seat next to her creaked. She opened one eye, then closed it again when she saw Jace. He seemed to understand that she didn't want to talk.

Through the next hour, the officers went in to see Paul, two at a time. His mother arrived and was rushed in.

She came out and walked over to Irene. "My dear," she said, and patted Irene's cheek. "Paul is asking for you."

Irene wished with all her heart she could say no. She realized what she needed to do, and it would be like tearing out her own heart. She knew it would hurt him, too.

Instead, she nodded and walked on numb legs to his room. She opened the door. His eyes were closed. She was able to convince herself that he was asleep. His lids drifted up and he met her gaze. Her heart sank.

Here goes. She entered the room. He smiled, a great open smile. When she didn't return it, his smile faded. Confusion twisted his face.

"Irene. I wanted to see you. Make sure you weren't hurt."

Her heart was beating so fast. "I'm fine. You saved my life."

"Irene, come here. I want to talk with you."

Her feet were leaden. She moved to the side of his bed.

"Today, when I knew you were in danger, I knew I had to tell you that I loved you. That I wanted a chance with you…"

She shook her head. No, no, no. This was all wrong. She had to stop it.

Paul's face paled. "You can't tell me you don't love me. I know you do."

He was right, she couldn't tell him that she didn't. "I won't lie to you. I have feelings for you. Strong ones. But I can't go through this again. I can't be a cop's wife again, living with the uncertainty. It would destroy me."

"Irene." Paul reached out his hand to her. His eyes swam with tears.

She couldn't stand it. Shaking her head, she backed up, then walked out of the room, tears on her cheeks. Her shoulders shook when she heard him call her name. She ignored it and kept walking, knowing Jace was at her side. His glance kept going between her and down the hall where his best friend lay.

Poor Jace. She hadn't meant to put him in this position, and yet she couldn't do anything about it. "Take me home, Jace."

His mouth tightened, but he nodded. He took her home and dropped her off. Their mother and her children greeted her.

She answered their questions without emotion, feeling empty inside.

She had left her heart at the hospital.

SEVENTEEN

Irene pulled into Gina Martello's driveway and shut off the engine. She sat for a moment, staring blindly out the front windshield. Her last client for the day had canceled, allowing her to leave work early. Her sons and her mother-in-law weren't expecting her for another thirty minutes. She could go in and grab the boys, and maybe they could pick up a pizza on the way home. It would be a special treat for them. Yes. That's exactly what she would do.

She didn't move.

Paul. Two weeks had passed since she'd left him in the hospital. Christmas was four days away.

What was he doing tonight? Was he still at work, neck-deep in a new case? She could picture him, strolling around the police station as if he had no cares, whistling the theme song for the Andy Griffith Show.

How she missed him.

He had said he loved her. His eyes had been filled with that love the last time she'd seen him. And pain. Pain from his wound, true. But even more pain because she had rejected him.

But it was the right move, wasn't it? After all, did she really need to risk her heart again?

Her mind flashed back to a conversation she'd had with Jace two nights ago. He'd told her she was being dumb, letting the past ruin her chances for love again.

"I just want to be happy," she'd shot back.

"Because you're so happy now?" he'd countered. "Really? Are you?"

She couldn't answer. It didn't matter. He kept talking. "When are you going to realize that we are always in danger of losing those we love? We have lost Dad, Ellie and Tony. We didn't have any choice about that. But you have a choice. Paul is still very much alive. Do you really want to lose him, too?"

Did she?

Too late.

The truth sank in deep. It was too late. She was already soul-deep in love with the man. How had it happened? She had tried to protect her heart, and it hadn't mattered in the end. She had fallen.

Now both of their hearts were broken.

Not to mention the suffering of her boys. Oh,

they didn't say anything. A mother knew when her children were sad, though. She could tell they missed Paul. He would have made a wonderful father for them.

Stop it! What's done is done.

Impatient with her maudlin thoughts, Irene got out of the car, slamming the door shut. And closing her mind to thoughts of Paul. Of his strength and courage. Of his gentleness. That deep voice…

Enough!

She stamped through the snow on the walkway up to the door and let herself in. She could hear muted voices in the playroom. An Italian aria was playing in the kitchen. She followed the music.

Gina was baking cookies.

A wave of love for her late husband's mother flooded her. The woman had become more than an in-law. She was a true friend. Just then, the older woman seemed to become aware of Irene and turned, a welcoming smile on her face.

"Irene! Did I lose track of the time?" Gina turned to glance at the clock on the wall.

"No, I got off early."

Gina started to speak, then she narrowed her eyes at Irene and pursed her lips.

Irene knew that look. The woman was dying

to say something and was trying to hold her tongue. "What?"

"What? What do you mean 'what'?"

Irene rolled her eyes. "Come on, Gina. You know you want to say something."

The woman held her tongue for another ten seconds before she gave in. "Ah, me. You know I love you like a dear daughter, Irene? I don't like to see you unhappy. Or the boys."

Irene walked over and kissed her cheek. "We're fine, Gina. Or we will be."

"You are in love with Tony's boss, Paul. I can see it."

Irene opened her mouth to deny it, but couldn't. Distress filled her. The last thing she wanted to do was cause her mother-in-law pain. How would the woman feel knowing she had let another man into her heart? Fearfully, she gazed at the woman.

Gina gave her a gentle smile in return. It was a bittersweet smile.

"Irene, my son loved you with all his heart. Until the day he died, you and the boys were his everything. I know you loved him, too." Irene's heart thumped hard in her chest. Where was this headed? Gina continued. "I will always miss my Tony. I wish he were here to see his sons grow. It breaks my heart to know he won't. But you are young. If God has given you a second chance at love, who are you to deny it? Or to deny my grandsons the blessing a good stepfather would bring?"

"But Gina," Irene choked out. "Paul is the chief of police. How can I love a cop again? How could I survive the worry, the pain again?"

Gina clucked her tongue. "Shame on you! Where is your faith? God will always see you through. You can't live without pain. Or love. That's life. Embrace it, Irene. It is a gift."

It's a gift.

Irene pondered and struggled with those words until Christmas Eve. Each day, each moment, the conviction grew inside her. She had made a mistake to reject Paul. He had a dangerous job, but being with him would be worth the risk. There was a hole in her heart without him at her side.

Was she too late?

She'd soon find out, she thought, as she pulled into the church parking lot for the late-night service. She arrived early. The choir performed Christmas music for an hour before the service began. Her boys had taken a late-afternoon nap so they would be able to last through the service. Paul was already there. She recognized his car the minute she pulled in. Her insides began to quake. Would she be able to ask him for another chance? And how would she handle it if he rejected her?

Jace and Mel pulled into the lot at the same time. Her mom had driven in with them. Together, the small group moved inside the church, alight with decorations and candles. People smiled and greeted them as they passed. Irene acknowledged each greeting, though she didn't stop. She had a goal in mind.

Paul was sitting near the front. Alone. Not for long.

Setting her jaw, Irene started to lead the group toward him. At first Jace looked startled, and then a satisfied smile settled over his face as he saw where she was headed. She ignored him. Nothing mattered other than getting to Paul. Her heart ached at the slump of his shoulders. She had put that there. He had taken many blows in life, but she had never seen him dejected. It was a posture she never wanted to see again.

She reached his row. He still hadn't looked up. Sucking in a deep breath, she started to enter.

Jace stopped at the row behind them and ushered their mother into it ahead of them. Melanie followed, holding a sleeping Ellie in her arms. Jace moved in after them. As he moved behind

Paul, he tapped his boss and best friend's left shoulder. Paul turned his head to see Jace.

Irene slipped into the seat beside him. Matthew looked around her and saw who was sitting there.

"Chief Paul!"

The exclamation brought Paul's head swinging around in shock.

His startled gaze connected with Irene's. He opened his mouth. Closed it again. Then he blinked his eyes, fast. And swallowed.

Overcome, Irene bit her lip. One tear slipped past her eyelids even though she tried to hold it back. Paul lifted a trembling hand and wiped it away.

She smiled. It was all she was capable of at the moment.

AJ and Matthew scooted passed her to hug Paul. He embraced them both. Then the boys repositioned themselves so one was on either side of him. Irene was forced to make room for Matthew. She didn't mind, though. The look of startled joy in Paul's eyes was all she needed.

They had yet to speak a word. Halfway through the service, Jace leaned forward and scooped Matthew up in his arms, settling the boy back with him. To her surprise, the child didn't fuss. Immediately, Paul moved closer to

Irene. Her breath caught as he took her hand in his.

He held her hand through the remainder of the service. Joy swirled through her at the touch. Every now and then, she squeezed his hand and he returned the gesture. Just to let her overwhelmed heart know that he was really there, accepting her and loving her back, despite the way she'd hurt him. God was so good. So faithful. Despite her weakness and her failings, He was giving her a second chance.

She was really here. Beside him.

He'd been a bear to be around the past few days. He was man enough to admit it and feel bad about it. He hadn't been tempted to whistle even once since he'd been stabbed. All because she was gone. He had been furious with her at first. He knew she loved him. He'd seen it in her expression in the ambulance. For a short while, he'd allowed himself to believe they had a chance.

Then she'd crushed him and walked away like what they had didn't matter.

And now she was here. And he was holding her hand. He squeezed again. She reciprocated, and his world righted itself. He hadn't thought much about it when Jace had sat behind him. He hadn't realized that Irene had slipped in beside him until he had heard Matthew. He'd never forget the way his whole being had seized up in joy and hope.

For the first time in almost a week, Paul felt whole again.

When the service ended, Paul looked back at Jace and raised his brows.

Jace grinned.

"Hey, munchkins. Why don't I take you home? If your mom gives me her keys, then Chief Paul can drive her home. Okay?"

Good old Jace. He understood him well.

"Why wouldn't Mommy drive us home?" Matthew scrunched up his nose and peered at his uncle.

"Don't be such a baby," AJ scolded. "Mommy and Chief Paul have adult things to talk about."

Matthew pushed out his lower lip. An eruption was imminent.

"Come on boys. We'll talk in the car."

With a few grumbles from Matthew, the others left. Paul hadn't missed the blush on Irene's face as she'd handed over her keys. They sat quietly for a few minutes as the others in the church began to drift out to their cars. The pastor came in to lock the doors.

When he saw Paul and Irene, he smiled. "Would you like me to come back in a few minutes to lock up?"

"That would be wonderful."

The pastor left them quietly.

Finally, it was just the two of them. It should have felt weird to have this conversation in a church. It didn't, though. Because he knew that God was with them in this moment, on this holy night. He wanted His blessing on them.

"Paul," Irene began in a hushed voice. "Oh, Paul, I was so stupid."

"Irene." He moved slightly away so that he could turn to her, raising his leg so his hip and thigh were against the back of the pew bench, his knee bent. She did the same. They sat facing each other, knee to knee. But he never released her hand. "I have missed you so much. Every day. I have to know. Did you change your mind? Because I don't think I could handle that kind of rejection from you again."

Tears misted her eyes. She nodded.

"I was so afraid," she admitted. "You were right. I did—do—love you. With all my heart. And it terrified me."

"Because of Tony." If his voice was a little flat, he couldn't help it. Tony had been a good man and a friend. He had also been a cop, and it had gotten him killed. Paul didn't think he could walk away from being a cop. Not because his love for Irene was shallow. It wasn't. His love for this sweet woman was overwhelming, part of his marrow. Being a cop, though, was what he believed his God called him to be. One didn't just abandon God's calling.

Irene flinched slightly at his tone. "Yes. Don't shut me out," she begged when he shifted slightly away. "I was wrong."

He stilled. Hope again took root.

"I thought that if I walked away from you, then I would be spared going through that kind of pain again. But I wasn't. I was hurting every day that we were apart. Even though you were still alive I was in pain because I was too stubborn to give you a chance. And I finally realized that I was wasting the time we do have. My brother reminded me that the next breath is never guaranteed."

Paul scooted in again, the emotion in his chest choking him. He reached out and ran his free hand through her glorious red hair. The soft strands sifted through his fingers. He'd thought he'd never be able to touch her hair again, to smell her light, floral perfume.

"Irene," he murmured when he could finally speak. "I have loved you since I was a senior in high school. I know I made mistakes with you. But I have never loved you more than I do right now."

The tears she'd been fighting finally broke through and rolled down her cheeks. He released her hands and gently wiped the wetness from her face. She was smiling by the time he was done.

"Paul Kennedy, I don't know why God has blessed me a second time, but I do love you." She leaned forward until their foreheads touched. They sat like that for several minutes.

A throat clearing made them break apart.

"Sorry, folks," the pastor said, "but I really do need to lock up."

Quietly, they stood, and Paul helped Irene into her coat. When she looked up at him, he couldn't resist stopping long enough to drop a chaste kiss onto her soft lips. She sighed.

The drive home was filled with murmured conversation. Paul didn't stay long after he dropped her off. Mostly because he had some planning to do for Christmas day. Jace being present was also a factor. He ignored his best friend's smirk as he kissed Irene quickly at the door and drove home.

He all but ran up the walkway and into his house when he arrived. Irene loved him!

Thank You, Jesus!

There's was no way he was going to be able to sleep now. He glanced at the clock. It was after ten. Well, as long as he had the energy...

He wrapped up the presents he had bought the boys last week.

Then he made a phone call to a friend. Yes, it was late at night, but the moment his old buddy heard what he needed, he was more than happy to assist. Paul hung up the phone and felt a moment of doubt. Did he dare take this step? Would it backfire? He'd find out in a few hours.

He hardly slept all night. Too keyed up. But by nine in the morning, he was done waiting. He knew that Irene and the boys would be off to her mom's at one o'clock, so he had time.

Irene let him in with a smile and a blush when he arrived. He understood. Even though the feelings between them had been growing for some time, their mutual acknowledgment was still shiny and new.

"Chief Paul!"

Laughing, Paul set the presents on the table in the hall and bent to scoop up the boys. What a joy they were! He chuckled again as their eyes widened when he handed them each their presents. He didn't usually give them gifts. Gifts were from family members. Irene shot him a speculative glance.

The boys were thrilled with their new remote-control cars. They hurled themselves at Paul, thanking him. Then they ran off to the kitchen to play with them. Snatching up Irene's hand, he pulled her into the living room. They could still hear the squeals and shouts coming from the other room, accompanied by barks from the dog.

Stopping in front of the tree, Paul faced Irene. She looked at him, her brow arched. How he loved her! Getting down on one knee, he drew out a ring. She gasped.

"My buddy Dex owns a jewelry store. I called him last night, and he opened the doors for me." He sucked in a deep breath. "Irene, I know it hasn't been a long time. But like I said, I have loved you for half of my life. These past two weeks without you have been some of the hardest I have ever known. I don't want to go another day without knowing that I have the right to finally call you mine."

"Oh!" Irene covered her mouth with her hand, but not before he glimpsed the smile that was coming out like the sun after a long, hard rain. It grew into a grin.

"Yes!" Irene held her shaking hand out to him. He put the ring right where it belonged. And then she was in his arms. Right where she belonged.

EPILOGUE

Irene stood in the bride room with her mother, Gina, Melanie, Maggie and Paul's sister, Cammie. Paul's mother was with Cammie's husband, Allen, keeping watch over the children while the women got ready for the ceremony. She couldn't believe this day was finally here. Of course, she and Paul hadn't had a long engagement. A little shy of three months. But it had felt like a lifetime, waiting for the day they could start their lives together.

"Do you have something borrowed?" Melanie asked.

Irene held her hand to her necklace. "Gina's lent me her pearls."

Gina Martello gave her a misty smile. "They look gorgeous on you."

Mel nodded. "And I gave you the earrings." The something blue.

Irene held her hand to her veil. "And Mom's veil." There was something old.

"Oh! Don't you dare make me cry!" her mother wailed softly. Her eyes were already watering even though there was a smile on her face.

"And your dress is something new." Mel grinned in satisfaction before hugging her sister-in-law gently. "Let's go get you married."

The ladies filed down into their positions. LaMar Pond policemen were present to escort the mothers to their seats before returning to stand near the groom. Claire Zerosky was lovely as she sat near the front, strumming on a harp. Seated near her was Miles, resplendent in his dress uniform, complete with its shiny sergeant insignia. He had agreed to interpret for Rebecca and Jess, who were both deaf. Rebecca and Jess were already seated with Seth. Irene grinned as she saw Rebecca blow Miles a kiss. He winked back at her.

It was time.

When Claire began the wedding march, Irene quivered. Excitement and joy burst through her as she watched the bridesmaids move towards the front. A very pregnant Maggie went first. Dan met her in the middle and escorted her the rest of the way. Cammie followed, to be met by Jackson. Next went Melanie, her maid of honor, to be met by Jace.

The guests let out a combined "aww" as

the flower girls made their way up the aisle. Cammie's four-year-old daughter waved at her grandmother as she walked, completely forgetting that she was supposed to be scattering the rose petals nestled in her basket. It was Maggie's daughter, Siobhan, however, who stole the show. Always willing to perform, she was in her element. She threw rose petals helter-skelter and waved with abandon. More than one guest ended up with petals in their hair. No one minded, though.

The smiles grew as Rory followed his twin sister, his face very serious under a mop of dark curls as he carried the wedding rings on a small satin pillow. The three youngsters were precious. Absolutely adorable.

But not, in Irene's eyes, as adorable as the two young men standing at either side of her. Jace had offered to walk her down the aisle. But when AJ and Matthew heard about it, they shut down the idea.

"She's our mommy," AJ had stated. "And Chief Paul will be our new daddy. It should be us. 'Cause we're gonna be a family."

She'd nearly come undone at those sweet words. Paul had cleared his throat and embraced the boys, one at a time. "I think you two would be the perfect choice. How 'bout it, Jace? Best man?"

Jace had wiped his own eye. "Yeah, man. I am anyway."

Now she nodded at her boys. While she held her bouquet in her hand, each little boy held on to an elbow. The guests that had smiled at Cammie and the twins grew teary eyed as Irene's sons walked her down the aisle to Paul.

Finally, she stood before her groom, breathless and expectant. She smiled through her own tears as she saw him blink. She wasn't the only one affected by the beauty of this moment. From now on, they would be together. More than that, her heart overflowed with gratitude that her sons, soon to be his children, too, would once again have an earthly father to guide them. She whispered a quiet prayer of gratitude to God. She knew Paul felt the same. Just the night before, he'd admitted that he was overwhelmed. Never had he believed he would be the recipient of such a gift. She made herself a promise that she would never take what they'd been blessed with for granted, and instead would cherish it every day for the rest of their lives.

The ceremony was exquisite. Irene listened with joy as Paul said his vows in his strong, deep voice. When it was her turn, she didn't hesitate. She repeated the words that would bind her to this brave man with vibrant intensity, meaning them from the depths of her soul. When the rings were in place and blessed, her heart grew so full she could barely breathe.

At last the time came when they were announced husband and wife.

"You may now kiss the bride."

The bride. His bride.

Paul cupped Irene's face in his hands as if it were the most precious thing in the world. She quivered with the anticipation of his kiss. When his lips touched hers, she sighed, melting into the kiss.

After all the heartache and despair they had both endured, God had brought them healing and love.

After several heartbeats, they drew apart and shared a smile meant only for each other.

The pastor indicated they should turn and face the congregation.

"I now present to you Mr. and Mrs. Paul Kennedy."

As their friends and family smiled and clapped, Paul and Irene faced the congregation with AJ and Matthew in front of them. Together, the four stood, a family at last.

* * * * *

*If you loved this book, don't miss
the other heart-stopping Amish adventures
from Dana R. Lynn's*
AMISH COUNTRY JUSTICE *series:*

*PLAIN TARGET
PLAIN RETRIBUTION*

*Find more great reads at
www.LoveInspired.com.*

Dear Reader,

When I first wrote about LaMar Pond, I had no idea where Paul's story would lead him. I knew I wanted to give him a happy-ever-after, but had no plans beyond that. As the characters of LaMar Pond have evolved, the story of Irene and Paul began to play out in my imagination.

Paul is a man who had once hit bottom and who has fought to conquer his problems. Along the way, he developed a strong faith. He is a man who has much to offer a woman. Even if he doesn't know it.

Irene has dealt with the horror of losing the husband she loved and raising their children by herself. Such a trial made her turn her back on God for a while, but He brought her back, loving her and showering His mercy upon her.

Irene and Paul are brought together by their shared quest to assist a child in need. As I wrote this story, I was reminded of how Jesus asks us to have the faith of a child.

I hope you enjoyed Paul and Irene's story. I hope to continue writing about the people in LaMar Pond. I love to hear from readers. You can email me at WriterDanaLynn@gmail.com or visit me online at www.danarlynn.com. I am also on Facebook and Twitter (@DanaRLynn).

Blessings,
Dana R. Lynn

Get 2 Free Books,
Plus 2 Free Gifts—
just for trying the Reader Service!